Tara Pammi

AN INNOCENT TO TAME THE ITALIAN

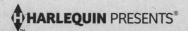

Recycling programs
for this product may
not exist in your area.

ISBN-13: 978-1-335-47846-7

An Innocent to Tame the Italian

First North American publication 2019

Copyright © 2019 by Tara Pammi

This edition published by arrangement with Harlequin Books S.A.

For questions and comments about the quality of this book, please contact us at CustomerService@Harlequin.com.

Printed in U.S.A.

"Tut, tut… Natalie, you disappoint me. The last thing I need in my life is a wife who wants love. I have nothing to give a wife. Just do your part, *si*?" Massimo mocked.

He waited for her to contradict him.

"And if I say no? If I tell your ex and your grandmother that it's all a big pretense?"

A spear of disappointment lodged in his chest. Could she truly be as innocent and inexperienced as she sounded? Did he really care if she was? "You won't do that."

"I just…"

"Be smart about this, Natalie." All humor fled his tone. "If I find you told me the truth about your financials, about this not being a job, then what do you have to lose? For once in your life, maybe you could use your interesting capabilities to make a living. Spend a few months in the lap of luxury in Milan. Pretend to be the fiancée of the most—"

"Arrogant, high-handed man on the planet? Sure, how hard can it be?"

"So?"

"Fine. I agree to your conditions."

"*Bene.*"

Tara Pammi can't remember a moment when she wasn't lost in a book—especially a romance, which was much more exciting than a mathematics textbook at school. Years later, Tara's wild imagination and love for the written word revealed what she really wanted to do. Now she pairs alpha males who think they know everything with strong women who knock that theory and them off their feet!

Books by Tara Pammi

Harlequin Presents

Conveniently Wed!

Bought with the Italian's Ring
Blackmailed by the Greek's Vows
Sicilian's Bride for a Price

The Drakon Royals

Crowned for the Drakon Legacy
The Drakon Baby Bargain
His Drakon Runaway Bride

Brides for Billionaires

Married for the Sheikh's Duty

Bound to the Desert King

Sheikh's Baby of Revenge

The Legendary Conti Brothers

The Surprise Conti Child
The Unwanted Conti Bride

Visit the Author Profile page
at Harlequin.com for more titles.

AN INNOCENT TO
TAME THE ITALIAN

For Jen—for talking me up when I'm down, for untangling complicated plots only we could come up with and for always being there to discuss how much we can push cranky, arrogant heroes. This book wouldn't have been possible without you.

CHAPTER ONE

"DID YOU FIGURE out why the security breaches keep happening? And how?"

Massimo Brunetti looked up from the three monitors on his desk in the lab that was the hub of his cyber security business. It was a high-security center with thumbprint access only.

A measure he'd taken at the age of sixteen when his father, Silvio, had still been living with them, a matter of self-preservation for Massimo to keep him out. Now, this was his tech center where his servers were stored and where he designed software worth billions.

Only his older half brother, Leonardo, who was currently scrutinizing everything, and their grandmother Greta's stepdaughter, Alessandra, had access. On the condition that they disturb him only at the threat of the building burning down or an equivalent emergency.

Greta wasn't allowed. Her emergency the last time had been an epic tantrum on his thirtieth birthday three months ago. The cause was that Leo and he were going to die childless, leaving the dynastic legacy of the Brunettis to perish with them.

She should know Massimo didn't give a damn about family legacies, especially theirs.

"We have a meeting scheduled for an update in a half hour, Leo," he said, without raising his head. "You know I do not like it when you barge in here."

"You've been locked up in here for the better part of a week." Leo's mouth pinched. "I can't hide it from the board any longer, Massimo. If it gets to the press that BCS had clients' financials open for any little Dark Net hacker to find... *Merda!*"

It would be a disaster of epic proportions.

"It's bad enough we lost that ten-billion-dollar contract," Leo finished.

Massimo rubbed his eyes with the heels of his hands, hoping to alleviate the pulsing prick of pain in his forehead. He *had been* cooped up in here for too long. "It's not my fault if people remember the trail of destruction Silvio left in his wake."

It had taken Leo and him close to fifteen years to restore their family company—a multi-billion-dollar finance giant, Brunetti Finances, Inc.—to its original glory. In fact, it was still a work in progress.

For Greta, it was the family legacy, the name Brunetti synonymous with its prestige. Even now, she could call out half the skyscrapers littered through Milan that had housed the main offices of Brunetti Finances through its two-hundred-year history.

For Leo and him, however, it was the satisfaction of building it up again, bigger and better, a force to be reckoned with, after their father had almost brought it to its knees.

But…for the last six months, more than one contract had fallen through at the last minute. In the first one, they had found that an accountant had leaked their bid details. In the second one, the subcontractor they'd hired had been bought off. Leaving an unholy mess on Leo's hands.

On top of that, there was this security breach Massimo had discovered a week ago in his own brainchild company, Brunetti Cyber Securities.

Someone was clearly targeting their business. The security breach was far too much a direct attack to ignore. If Silvio wasn't being monitored 24/7 at a clinic with no resources at hand and no communications beyond Leo, they would know the culprit was him. Their father, once they had grown taller, bigger and stronger than him, despised being powerless.

"Are you sure Silvio's the only enemy we have?" Leo asked, cocking an eyebrow at his brother. "What about your recent fling? She's certainly making a lot of noise."

"Gisela and I are done. Four months ago now." Massimo let his displeasure show on his face. Leo had no business delving into his personal matters.

"*Sì*, you and I know that. Does the daughter of the most powerful banking tycoon in Italy know that? *Maledizione*, Massimo, the woman calls *me* now."

The pain behind his eye intensified. If everything hadn't been going so wrong, Massimo would have laughed at his brother's expression.

Leo didn't even give out his number to his own mistress. Who was, very conveniently, a supermodel who had a shot at the end of the world, with an expiry date of two more months, if Massimo's calculations were right. The last one had been a CEO who met his brother once every two weeks for six months. Before that, had been a photojournalist studying migration patterns of an exotic bird species in Antarctica who went into hibernation for about ten months out of a year.

Leo seemed to have the algorithm for the best kind of mistress all figured out—distance, just as ruthless as him and ambitious. All his relationships ended on amicable footings, too.

It wasn't that Massimo wanted a cold and clinical relationship like that. He just didn' have the time or the energy for a deeper one. And he wouldn't for the next twenty years at least. He doubted he knew what deep, meaningful relationships looked like, anyway. His mother and Silvio—it had been a war. Fought by her, for his sake.

"You need to do whatever is needed to make her understand," Leo added. "Do not antagonize her father in the process."

Massimo hated when Leonardo was right. "I'll take care of it."

It had been a stupid move tangling with the selfish, spoiled socialite Gisela Fiore. But after the months he'd spent designing his latest product—an e-commerce tool and its subsequent release hitting ten billion in revenue—he'd needed to play. Hard.

Which Gisela excelled at, according to her reputation. The *only* thing she excelled at. A torrid two-week affair had ensued. At the end of which, Massimo had been itching to get back to work. As was *his* reputation.

Except Gisela was still sending him alarmingly disturbing texts full of threats followed by sobbing messages. When she wasn't camping outside the Brunetti brothers' office building.

"Do you want to hear about the hacker or not?" he challenged Leo.

"Please."

"I found the trail last night. I also figured out how he gained access through the multiple firewalls I built. Both times."

"Two times?" Leo asked with cutting focus to the gist of the vast problem on their hands.

"*Sì.*"

"*Cristo*, you're a freaking genius, Massimo. How is that even possible?"

It wasn't arrogance that made Massimo nod. Computers were his thing. The one thing he was the master of. "The hacker is obviously extremely talented. A true genius, no doubt."

Leo's curse exploded in the basement. A few minutes later, his brother was all business again. "But you have the proof tying it to this person, right?"

"*Sì.* I used the bots to piggyback onto the malware he—"

"Normal people words, Massimo, *per favore*," his brother said with a smile, for the millionth time in their lives. "Words a small brain like mine can understand."

As always, a spurt of warmth jolted through his veins at Leo's joke. His brother was no fool. But when Massimo had been at his lowest, Leo, with his words, full of concern and praise, had urged him toward realizing his full potential. "I have proof. I have even triangulated the hacker's physical location. New York."

"That's fantastic. I can arrange for a meeting with the commissioner in a half hour. He'll get the cybercrime division involved. We'll have the hacker behind bars by tonight and the identity of whoever orchestrated this—"

"*No*. I don't want the *polizia* involved. Not yet."

"What? Why the hell not?"

"I've already figured out a cyber club where this hacker plays. I've established contact."

"Contact with the hacker? Why?"

Massimo shrugged. He couldn't exactly put it into words—curiosity, thrill, even a certain amount of camaraderie. The hacker intrigued him. "I want to get to know him. Learn how he operates."

"*Dios mio*, Massimo, he breached our security. Twice."

"*Essattemente!* He could do it again and again. You have to admit that there's something…fishy about the whole thing. None of the clients' financials were leaked. I have bots working everywhere they could be sold, like black markets, on the Dark Net. They haven't surfaced anywhere.

"It's as if the hacker is taunting me, playing with me. He's hard to pin down."

"What are you suggesting?"

"Let me develop a relationship with him. Let me get into his head. When I know how he works, how he's doing it, I'll spring the trap."

"I want your word that he won't hit our servers again."

"You losing faith in me, Leo?" he taunted, that resentment in him finding voice. Reminding him that Massimo wasn't still the always sick runt their father went off on whenever he was on one of his frequent alcoholic tirades. That he wasn't the younger brother running to his older brother's arms to hide from his father. That he was the computer genius who'd designed products that generated billions in revenue.

Leo paused at the high-tech sliding doors, frowning.

"Give me a week and I'll give you the hacker, his life story and the proof of his illegal activities, all tied up with a bow like a Christmas present."

"A week. At the most," Leo pushed back. "I want him behind bars."

One week later

Massimo stood outside the cyber club exit—a metal door of undistinguishable color at the rear of a dilapidated building in one of the run-down neighborhoods of Brooklyn. A far cry from his penthouse that overlooked Central Park that he'd left behind an hour ago.

March snow carpeted the parking grounds in the dark alley, thankfully suppressing the odors emanating from the vast trash containers that stood two feet from him.

The hacker, he'd found, was very much a creature of habit. Unlike Massimo, and much against the popular culture's rendition of a chaotic, free-spirited genius. Two evenings a week, the hacker came to this club, at exactly eight minutes past nine p.m. and stayed for exactly forty-three minutes. Before going completely off-line.

Like a junkie allowing himself a very strictly mandated and measured fix.

Massimo hadn't found him anywhere else.

Which meant all Massimo had had were two sessions of forty-three minutes to get to know how the guy operated. And he had. Hackers were a mysterious and antisocial bunch, and yet boastful, too, especially someone at the level at which this particular one operated. All he'd needed to do was compliment him on his modification of a security challenge posed by the master of the club. He hadn't quite owned up to the breach but the connection had been made.

His heart fluttering against his rib cage like a caged bird, Massimo tucked his hands into the pockets of his trench coat. Adrenaline hadn't hit him this hard since the release of his latest software product. No, that wasn't true. The last time he'd been this excited had been when he'd shored up the tunnel this very same hacker had created into BCS.

The metallic whine of the heavy door made his spine lock. Buffeted by the collar of his coat against the harsh wind, Massimo watched a slight figure swathed in black from head to toe, a dark contrast against the snow clinging to every crevice and roof of the building, walk down the steps.

The howl of the frigid wind pushed the hood away from the figure's face, revealing a delicate jawline with a wide, plump mouth. A too-sharp nose and a high forehead. Broad but sharp cheekbones. A pointed chin.

Slender shoulders held an almost boyish figure with long legs swathed in black denim and knee-high boots.

Jet-black hair, wild and curly, the only thing that betrayed the fact that she was a woman. No, the soft fragility, the sharply delicate bones, couldn't be mistaken for a man.

A painfully young, delicately beautiful woman.

It couldn't be her... This fragile young woman couldn't be the hacker that had taken down his firewall, could she? Couldn't be the diabolically intelligent computer genius that Massimo had been chatting up for the last week. The hacker that Leonardo wanted behind bars *pronto*. The one who'd kept him up for a fortnight now, given him sleepless nights...

Not a single one of his girlfriends had ever done it.

He laughed, a harsh bark that sounded loud in the silence.

Like a deer caught in the headlights, the hacker's feet frozen in the snow, her face turned toward him.

Brown eyes with long lashes alighted on his face and paused. He saw her swallow, felt that gaze dip to his mouth and trail back up to meet his eyes. A soft sound, almost like a kitten's sigh, filled the silence around them. Followed by the soft treads of her boots as she returned to the car.

No, he wasn't wrong.

He'd even had a quick chat with the hacker from his car before he'd stepped out. He...or *she* had been inside that building. On an impulse, Massimo grabbed his tablet from the car and sent a quick message through the chat boards.

It wasn't a sure thing since the hacker never used the chat boards outside of the cyber club. And yet, Massimo had teased him today with a glimpse of the new security software he was building for Gisela's father's company. He knew the hacker had been intrigued, had even stayed beyond the forty-three minutes he usually allowed himself.

Vitruvian Man: I can show you the double encryption layer for the new design.

His heart raced. *Dios mio*, he felt like a teenage boy waiting for his first kiss.

The woman paused, pulled her phone out from the coat jacket. Massimo realized what it meant to wait with bated breath.

His tablet sent out a soft chirp that sounded like a fire alarm in the dark silence.

Her reply shone up at him.

Gollum: Not tonight, thank you. My time's up. Maybe next time.

The message flashed on his screen and a smile curved his mouth, a flare of excitement running through his veins.

So polite, he'd thought during his chats with her. A certain softness buried even in the software jargon in contrast to the ruthlessness with which she'd attacked his firewalls.

It was her.

She was the hacker he'd been chasing, the hacker who it seemed was truly Massimo's match.

In the few seconds it took him to accept this new discovery, and course-correct his strategy for her, she'd reached her car.

His long legs ate up the distance. The tightening of her shoulders made him stay a few steps from her. He didn't want to scare her. Not yet.

"Why Gollum?" he said, keeping his tone soft, even as anger and excitement roped through him. "Why not Aragorn, or Gandalf the Wizard?"

She turned. Her eyes ate him up, her breath coming in short, shallow spurts that had nothing to do with the cold. "I don't know what you're talking about."

When she made to pull the driver's door to her beaten down Beetle, he crowded her. Still not touching.

The subtle scent of lavender filled his breath, a jarring thread of softness that made him breathe hard. He lifted his phone, the screen showing the chat boards. "I know who you are. I have proof of what you did to Brunetti Cyber Securities. Every last bit."

The smile faded from his face just as the innocence dropped from hers.

The pointed chin lifted up, the expression in her eyes clear and sharp. "What do you want?"

He let the full power of his fury settle into his words. "Your purse, please."

She looked at the sea of white snow around them.

"There's nowhere to run. Nowhere to hide. I recommend doing as I ask."

Slowly, she pulled a wallet out of her back pocket and handed it over.

"Natalie Crosetto," he said loudly. The name reverberated in the silence, and he breathed a sigh. "You've led me on a merry chase all over the internet, Ms. Crosetto, and now, I will run this game. We will go back to my hotel and you'll explain to me why you've been attacking my systems."

"No!" She took a deep breath. "You're a stranger. You can't expect me to let you just…kidnap me!"

"What do you suggest, then?"

"My home. Please. Tomorrow morning."

"I didn't take a trip over the Atlantic to let you escape me once I found you. We'll go to your home if that offers you a modicum of security. You're free to keep your cell phone and dial the police if you feel a threat to your person at any point, even.

"But you'll answer each and every one of my questions and you will do so tonight."

That stubborn chin raised even as her mouth quivered. Scared, and yet she challenged him. "Or else what?"

"Or else you'll be behind bars tonight. I will even let you call the cops yourself. And you'll stay there for the next decade, if I have anything to say about it."

CHAPTER TWO

NATALIE CROSETTO STARED at the man lounging on her couch—a soft but old piece she'd picked up at thrift store last month—as if he were a king sitting on his golden throne, surveying a subject brought up for judgment.

Her.

Sweat gathered on her upper lip and the nape of her neck. The tremors that had taken over her body wouldn't abate.

Jail. He could send her to jail...which meant any chance of her getting custody of Frankie would go up in flames. Christ, why the hell had she let Vincenzo talk her into this? What would happen to her brother if she ended up in jail? No, God, no...

"Head down between your knees. And deep breaths, Ms. Crosetto." He stood to give her room to sit.

She automatically followed the commanding voice and bent her torso down. The blackness taking over her vision faded, breath rushing into her lungs with the force of a storm. In, out. In, out.

Panic receded, bringing rational thought in its wake. She couldn't count on Vincenzo coming to her rescue. Not when she didn't know how to contact him beyond a number she could text. Not when she didn't know what the stranger would do with that information.

She had no one to count on but herself. As always.

Still keeping her head down, she went over the jumble of thoughts in her head, unraveling each one.

She'd covered her tracks very well, the first time. This man…he'd have never tracked her by that. But then, she'd tunneled through the firewalls a second time. Albeit with utter reluctance at Vincenzo's behest. That had been her mistake.

Still, the man on the other end had to be a genius to have tracked her. With unlimited resources. And not just online but all the way here. To show up right outside the cyber club, to taunt her with that text, to trap her so neatly…

She looked up and panic threatened to overwhelm her again.

A stranger in her apartment.

Her sanctuary. Her only safe place from the cruel world outside. She had never even invited Vincenzo here.

God, what a mess.

She pushed a hand through her hair and tugged at it. Her scalp tingled, the pain dispersing the remnants of panic. She'd survived worse situations. She'd find a way out of this, too.

First, she needed to protect herself from him. Needed to get him out of her home.

From the trench coat he'd discarded to the crisp black suit, the cuff links at his wrists, which she'd guess to be platinum, all the way to the handmade black leather shoes he was tapping on her cheap linoleum floor—he was expensively dressed. She might not know all of Vincenzo's background but he had expensive tastes.

This man was no different.

Even his jet-black haircut, carefully piled artistically at the top of his head, looked expensive, catering to the high cheekbones and forehead, sharpening those features even more. He was no mere IT officer or a hound sent to track her down.

Even if she could get away from him, he or his higher-ups would come after her. Again. Neither could she be a fugitive for the rest of her life. And yet…the need to take control of the situation was overwhelming.

Keeping her eyes on his lean frame lounging against the opposite wall, Nat pushed herself to her feet. Shuffling her feet, she slowly reached for the baseball bat she kept next to the bookshelf. One of the numerous things she'd been collecting to make the tiny apartment a home for Frankie.

The wood felt solid in her hand as she lifted it.

"Drop it, Ms. Crosetto," he said in a mildly bored tone.

She couldn't. Not for the life of her.

For a man who topped a couple of inches over six feet, he moved with a grace and economy she couldn't believe. In two seconds, his lean frame was crowding her. A gasp fell from her mouth when his fingers wrapped around her wrist, forcing her to drop the bat. The *thunk* of it hitting the floor reverberated in the small space. With a firm grip, he pushed her arm behind her until her upper body arched toward him. Her skin tingled where he held her tightly, but not hurting her.

Head falling back against the wall of his chest, she looked up at him.

And the impact of the man beneath the expensive clothes hit her hard. Hit her in places she didn't want to think about in front of him.

Intelligence and something else glimmered in his gaze. Dark shadows hung under his penetrating gray eyes. His sharp nose had a small dent right in the middle. His mouth…wide, the bow of the upper lip carved, it was so…sexy.

Awareness rushed in through her blood, settling into a warm throb in her lower belly. A shocking heaviness in her breasts.

Her breaths became shallow. He stood so close that she could see the slight flare of his pupils, the harsh breath he pulled in before his fingers tightened on her wrist.

She wouldn't be surprised to discover he was one of those male models that seemed to have been born with the perfect bone structure. To whom everything in life came easy. Women at their feet and millions in their bank account.

"Do not dig yourself a deeper hole, Ms. Crosetto."

The arrogance in his tone banished the airy lethargy in her limbs. "You're in my home. You cornered me and intruded into my apartment. You—"

He released her instantly. Stepped back, and Nat felt air rushing back into her lungs. "I mean you no harm. Not physically at least. Also, may I remind you that you invited me into your home. And I—" he cast a dismissive look around her living room, that upper lip turned up into a sneer "—expected to find you in something better than this hovel. Didn't you get paid enough for the hacking job to upgrade from…this?"

She rubbed the sensitive skin at her wrist, more to rid herself of the warmth he left behind than because of any hurt. And to stop herself from smacking the distaste off his curling mouth. "I've no idea what you're talking about."

He sat back onto the couch, leaning his arms onto his long legs, every movement utterly masculine. And yet graceful. "How much did you get paid for taking down the firewalls at BCS?"

"You're mistaking me for someone else. I'm nothing but a low-level clerk at a cheap easy-loan company in Brooklyn."

He rubbed a long finger over his left temple. "No more lies, *per favore*." His accent sent shivers down her spine that had nothing to do with fear.

When he looked up at her, impatience swirled in his gaze. "Let's cut through the innocent act. Now that I have your actual identity, it will take me no time at all to find your financials, every personal record, from your date of birth to how often you visit your ATM."

In a bare, few words that sent all her assumptions of him grounding into dust, he rattled off, step by step, the date and time to the exact second when she had bypassed his security measures and brought down the firewalls at BCS. And not as if he had learned it by rote.

"So, you're not just a pretty, rich boy?"

He stilled, except for raising a brow on that gorgeous face. She could swear his eyes twinkled but then she didn't trust herself right now. "A pretty, rich boy, huh? Remind me to tell my older brother that, *si*? He'll find it amusing."

Nat could only stare.

"I don't think you comprehend the trouble you're in."

"I'm terrified at the trouble I'm in. You've no idea what…" She took a deep breath and pushed her shaking hands behind her. "But attacking even when you're cornered is sometimes the only defense you've left in life."

Something like interest dawned in his eyes before he went on to outline how he'd tracked her signature to the cyber club, made contact with her. How he'd triangulated her physical location. How when he'd given her a small opening in the guise of his latest tech, she'd all but opened herself to him.

Her foul curse rang like a gunshot.

"It was clever. No, not clever. It was sheer genius. But you made a mistake. You—"

"I came back a second time without masking my trail," she finished, a knot of tension in her throat. He had her. Nicely trapped. Without doubt.

"Yes, that. But you also shouldn't have returned to the scene of your crime—that cyber club. Why did you?"

She shrugged, refusing to give any more information. Like how every inch of her had been fascinated by his diabolical talent after he'd patched the tunnel she'd created. How she didn't even really have the kind of technology on hand to pull off something like this, how even membership to the cyber club had been gained for her by Vincenzo.

"Why are you talking to me instead of turning me in, then?" she challenged boldly, even as fear coated her skin with cold sweat.

If only she could somehow contact Vincenzo...

"How and why."

"What do you mean?" she said sharply, feeling as if she was a prisoner whose execution had been stayed.

He looked at his fingers and then up. Uncrossed his legs and then crossed them again. Pulling the material of his tailored trousers upward. She'd never realized how distracting a man's powerful thighs could be. "I want to know how you did it. My firewalls, every bit of technology I design, is cutting edge, the best in the world. What you did should have been...impossible."

"You're dangling jail time over my neck as a sword because your ego got dented?" The words pushed out of her. "You and I both know I didn't touch a single client's financials. I...didn't *steal* anything. I'm not a thief. In any sense of the word."

"Which brings me to the second question. Why attack the security, bring down the firewalls...something that would have taken you days, if not to steal millions worth of financial info—"

"Five hours," she chimed in, and could have kicked herself. Damn it, where the hell was her sense of self-preservation? What was it about this man that pushed all the wrong buttons in her?

A stillness came over him. He rotated his neck on

his shoulders with that casual masculine elegance. But this time, Natalie saw through it. He was shocked. It was clear in the pinched look around his mouth when he cleared his throat and said, "You did it in five hours?"

"Yes."

If she could trust her judgment right then, Nat would have called the expression in his eyes excited. No…fascinated. He sounded fascinated and thrilled, his body containing a violent energy. More than angry that someone had attacked his design.

This was personal to him, too, this security breach she'd caused. She had to use that to her benefit, to persuade him to be lenient with her.

But she didn't trust herself right then, didn't know if she could pull it off. Not when he distracted the wits out of her. Jesus, the man held her future in his palm.

"How long did it take you the second time?"

"Fourteen hours. I… You made it much more complicated and I was under…duress."

Another smile, this one flashing his perfect white teeth, the warmth of it reaching his eyes. Nat blinked at the sheer beauty of the man. Dark skin at his throat contrasted against his white shirt. "Nice to know I'm not the only one who gives in to their ego. I had you penned right."

"You don't know anything about me," she whispered, a sane defense for once.

"I knew enough to put a tracker on the malware you introduced when you came back the second time. I have bots scouring through every black market, in case you stole the financials. I'll find out if you're part of a hacking syndicate. Any money you took for the job, I'll find the financial trail."

"There won't be any." Thank God she'd refused Vincenzo's financial offer. Thank God she'd retained some of her moral sensibilities. Her life had been too much of a bitch for her to afford them. But she'd refused. Because she hadn't wanted to benefit from illegal activity. "You'll see that I have two thousand and twenty-two dollars in my checking account and credit cards with over nine thousand dollars in debt. I live in this hovel, as you call it. I don't own a car. And most weeks, I live on ramen. I didn't make any money on this. It wasn't a job. I'm not... My services aren't for sale."

"So why do it? If it had been just the one time, I'd have assumed you had chickened out at the sheer scope of what you'd done and its consequences. But to come back..." He raised a hand when she opened her mouth. "Think carefully before you decide on an answer, Ms. Crosetto. And stick to the truth, if you can, *si*?

"I'm on a deadline to submit the security designs for a major project and I'm grouchy when I'm pulled away from my lab. Forget the fact that my older brother is breathing down my neck for not just having thrown you in jail when I first found you. One wrong word and I'll take his advice."

Sweat rolled down between her shoulder blades. A torrent of lies came and fell away from Nat's mouth. "I..." She swiped her tongue over her lips. Truth, as much as she could afford, was her only option. "I had no intention of stealing anything. I...have been stupid but I'm not greedy. I'm not a thief...by profession," she added at the last second.

His arrogant gaze bore through her. "I'm waiting, Ms. Crosetto."

"I did it on a challenge." It was the last answer he'd been expecting from his shocked expression. "I... Someone in the club issued a challenge."

"Who?" he demanded instantly, clearly not buying it.

"I don't know. All I gathered is that BCS's security was unbeatable. That your security guy's a genius. That he...no one could ever bring down his firewalls. I...

"I was foolish enough and egotistic enough to want to beat it. Not to prove anything to anyone. Just for myself."

"And the second time?"

"Hubris." This time, she was relieved to speak the truth. "You closed the tunnel minutes after I created it. It shouldn't have been possible. What you did the second time to put them up—to try to bring it down—it was a high." She'd constantly moaned about how wrong it was with Vincenzo, but it hadn't stopped her. He'd known how much she'd wanted to do it.

How exhilarating she found it to pit her mind against the security expert at BCS.

"Once I started, I... I lost the little sense I seem to have been born with. I... I swear, I'll never do it again. I... I've never done this before. Please, you've got to believe me."

"It's not that simple, Ms. Crosetto."

"Why not? You said—"

"I don't trust that brain of yours. I can't just...let you walk free."

She reached for the wall behind her, her knees giving out. Fear felt like shards of glass in her throat. "You'll send me to jail?"

He looked at her with a thoughtful expression, as if she were a bug under a microscope he was wondering whether to crush or not. He studied the beads of sweat over her upper lip. The shivers spewing over her entire body. "*No.* But I'm not letting you go, either."

"What does that mean?"

"You'll accompany me to Milan."

She shook her head, trying to swim through the emotions barreling through her. Fear and hope knotted painfully in her stomach. "I can't leave the country. I have… responsibilities."

"You should have thought of them before you decided to embrace the criminal life. Until I get to the bottom of this, until I decide what to do with you, you'll be my…guest. If you give me your passport, I'll arrange for travel immediately. I can't let you out of my sight and I do not like the idea of—"

"That's kidnapping!" Nat broke through his casual planning. "You're kidnapping me."

He didn't even blink. "The alternative is jail, Ms. Crosetto. There's too much at stake to magnanimously forgive you." He turned to his tablet, as if the topic was done. "Pack your things. We leave as soon as possible."

"I can't just… I have to tell someone that I'm leaving the country."

"A boyfriend? Perhaps the man who put you up to this?"

"No one did," she repeated, biting away Vincenzo's name at the last second.

This man was dangerous, in more than one way.

More than panic shimmied through her veins as his gaze touched her face. "My job, my... I don't even know who you are. What if you were a serial killer? A human trafficker? A harvester of organs who's salivating at the thought of getting his hands on my body?"

His hands on her body... What was wrong with her?

This time, there was no doubting the twinkle in his eyes. Or the languid heat flaring beneath.

Nat stepped back at the mere thought of what that meant. The last thing she needed was an...attraction between them. She knew squat about men. And less than squat about ambitious, ruthless, gorgeous men like her accuser. "Criminals, Ms. Crosetto, dead or alive, however diabolically clever—" his gaze raked her from top to toe and dismissed her in the same breath "—are not my type." He couldn't sound more upper class, refined and sophisticated, if he tried.

Everything she wasn't.

"But since I do not want a hysterical female on my hands on a long transatlantic flight, I'll tell you." He looked around her tiny living room, frowned and then settled those broad shoulders onto the wall behind him. The action pushed his hips and thighs away from the wall, highlighting the lean masculinity of the man. Every gesture, every movement of his, called all her senses to attention.

"I'm Massimo Brunetti, the cyber security genius you took on with such ease. And since I won't let you near an electronic device in the near future, I'll also give you the Google version, *sì*?

"I founded Brunetti Cyber Securities a decade ago when I was nineteen. I'm also the CTO for Brunetti Finances, an international finance giant. My brother, Leonardo, is the CEO. That's the one who wants you behind bars *pronto*.

"Our family, if you hadn't realized already, is old power and wealth, the kind of European dynasty others try to emulate unsuccessfully," he added, with nothing of the pride that was in his tone when he spoke of his security company. "So, yes, far more than your average pretty, rich boy who likes to have his way. Proceed with caution, *sì*?

"Also, I'll allow you one single call and you'll make it in front of me."

CHAPTER THREE

LACK OF SLEEP made Nat grit her eyes as dawn painted the New York sky beautiful shades of pink and orange. Unlike the light pollution that dimmed its shine in the city, the sky here in the country that she'd been driven into at three a.m. in a tinted limo, her sad little bag in hand, was gorgeous. The private airstrip was a hubbub of activity.

Massimo Brunetti…that name and all the power, wealth and reach that came with it had kept Natalie up all night.

She had Googled him the moment Vincenzo had mentioned BCS to her. Him and his CEO brother, Leonardo Brunetti. If Massimo was the brains behind Brunetti Finances, Leonardo was the heart. Cut in the same cloth as Massimo, ruthless when wielding his power, but much more socially active among the glitterati of Milan. The face of their business, the man who flashed his teeth at his enemies, brought in investors, managed the funds, while Massimo built brilliant software that brought in billions of revenue.

"Powerful men make powerful friends or enemies,"

Vincenzo had said, when she'd asked if he knew them. "A small favor," he'd called it. *Easy for her incisive mind.*

"Can you bring down BCS's security, Natalie?"

When she had argued that she couldn't risk anything criminal, she could never go down that path again, he had clasped her hand.

"I'd let nothing happen to you, *cara mia.* Find a flaw, bring it down. Nothing more. I'll not ask you to retrieve anything you discover, if you do crack it. Nothing to steal. Just find a weakness in the system."

"Then why?"—the only question she'd even thought to ask.

"Let's just say I have my eyes on the man who built it. I need to know if he's as good as they say. Not a single hacker I've hired so far has been able to get through."

And that had been his lure and she'd more than happily taken the bait.

She could've refused. He hadn't insisted on it. He hadn't called it as a return on all the favors he'd done for her and Frankie. He hadn't once, in the ten years since they'd met, mentioned how he'd saved her from a bullying foster parent, or from a wretched future in the juvie system. He hadn't mentioned not turning in Nat herself when he'd caught her stealing his wallet the first time they had met.

And yet, she'd done it.

Now she wondered at the questions she should've asked then.

What did Vincenzo have against Massimo?
Why this particular man?

Why his company?

Why had Vincenzo targeted the brainchild of tech genius Massimo Brunetti?

Instead, she'd thrown caution to the wind, given in to her one weakness and risked everything.

She hadn't even been able to reach Frankie during the one call Massimo had allowed her. While he'd watched her like a hawk circling a carcass, Natalie had left a message that she was going out of the country for a friend's sudden wedding, freeloading on the chance. That she would be out of coverage for a while but would call when she could. Her brother knew what a cheapskate she was.

"You're quite the storyteller, Ms. Crosetto," Massimo had said in his delicious Italian accent, all sleep mussed before he'd rushed her out of her apartment in the middle of the night, to collect their documents.

Nat pressed her fingers around the coffee cup in her hand—no rest-stop diesel-like coffee for Mr. Pretty Rich Boy. The dark roast felt like heaven on her tongue, anchoring her.

Her spine straightened against the limo as she heard Massimo step out on the other side. His security detail—one broad six-and-half-footer—and his two assistants: a thin man in his twenties with thick glasses and messed-up curly hair. What she'd expected the computer genius to look like—not the sleek, lean, sex-on-legs stud that was Massimo, shame on her prejudice… And the second one—a woman with a dark complexion, in her forties—followed him while he spoke into his cell phone.

Coffee forgotten, Nat watched him with wide eyes

as he walked back and forth in front of her speaking in rapid Italian that she couldn't understand a word of. After every other sentence, he paused, looked at her, and then started again.

Suit jacket gone, three buttons of the white dress shirt undone, that stylishly cut hair all rumpled up from his stint on her couch, he should've looked disheveled. At least a little tired. After all, he'd traveled across the Atlantic the previous day.

Instead, the stubble that coated his jaw and his upper lip, the V of his shirt glinting olive against the white of it, the snug fit of his trousers against lean hips—he was an erotic fantasy given form. The assault on her senses that had begun when she'd found him on her couch, trousers pulled up tight against powerful thighs, shirt equally snug against his shoulders, long lashes fanning against his sharp cheekbones... Her heart hadn't still recovered from it.

And then while she'd stared at him like an enthralled idiot, he'd opened those gray eyes. For just a second, there had been something in his eyes. Something that made liquid desire float through her veins. Before he sat up with his ubiquitous cell phone attached to his ear.

"The jet is ready. Let's go."

That was all he'd said to her, before bundling her into the limo. Coffee had been acquired on the way.

When she'd refused, he'd frowned. "Drink up, Ms. Crosetto. I need you awake and alert."

She'd tensed so hard her shoulders hurt. "Why?"

"Don't worry. I'm not going to ask you to breach the security of another company."

She'd immediately relaxed and then cursed herself when a shrewd light dawned in his eyes. Afraid he'd see even more, more than what she'd already betrayed, she'd looked away.

"I want to know exactly how you were able to create that tunnel through the firewall. Both the first and the second time. Each and every step. I want to also know of any other ways you can breach BCS's security. All the truth, Ms. Crosetto. Not just the convenient parts.

"If I even get a sniff of duplicity from you, you'll wish I had sent you to prison in your own country."

Even the wonderful aroma of coffee had felt like poison then.

The threat still ringing in her ears, she swallowed when he beckoned her from the foot of the air stairs. The arrogance of the man scraped her raw. She'd survived the cruelty and negligence of a foster care system that was supposed to protect her, the heartbreak of knowing that she wasn't good enough, just yet, to be her younger brother's family.

No way was she going to let Massimo Brunetti control her with the threat of incarceration. No man was going to make her live in fear every day, not after everything she'd been through. Not this easily.

And just like that, an idea began to percolate in her mind. Her shoulders straight, she tilted her chin and walked toward him with confidence.

The narrowing of his eyes made her smile.

Yep, she'd do what he asked of her, but she'd do it on her terms.

* * *

"Call the cops if you'd like. But I'm not getting on that plane. Not until you hear me out."

Massimo disconnected his call with Leo, Natalie's husky voice filled with determination sliding over his skin like a sensuous whisper. That same voice whispering at his ear, after a night spent in bed together, limbs heavy around each other, those dark brown eyes languid with sated desire... His imagination fired up the picture faster than he could breathe.

Dios mio, of all the women to spur this insta-lust in him...she was the worst choice.

He wanted to blame the last six months of his self-imposed celibacy for it. But then, after the fiasco with Gisela, he'd been a little bit disgusted with himself. He should've known better than to play with a spoiled princess.

He'd been more than a little tired of playing the same old game of chasing a woman just for sex. He had nothing more to give right now. Not at this point in his life.

And now Leonardo had informed him that Greta had been pulled into the whole mess with Gisela. His *nonni* had decided that Gisela would make a suitable bride for the scion of the Brunetti dynasty, that she was rich enough, sophisticated enough and blue-blooded enough to spawn the next generation of Brunettis.

Which was happening...*never*. But it did mean handling Gisela and, now, his *nonni* without giving offense to the former and hurting the second.

Of all the messes...

"Mr. Brunetti? Did you hear me? I'm not—"

He turned slowly, bracing himself. Still, the up-tilted chin and the wide brown eyes packed a punch.

This morning, she'd dressed in a light green-and-black sweater dress that hugged her slender frame, pointing out curves he'd missed last night. The loose neckline kept sliding off her shoulder showing glimpses of silky skin that beckoned his touch.

The dress ended beneath her buttocks—he'd seen enough when she'd walked ahead of him toward the limo, the knee-high leather boots displaying long legs that went on for miles. The mass of her black curls was pulled away into a tight knot at the top of her head, but in no way contained. Thick stray curls kept framing her face and she blew at them. A nervous tell that had made him smile in the limo. High forehead and a sharp nose only emphasized her gaunt face.

He frowned at the increasing appeal she held for him.

She wasn't the lush, curvaceous beauty he usually went after. Neither was she, he was sure, the experienced type he preferred, the way she'd jumped every time he came near. Women who owned their sexual desires usually meant uncomplicated but pleasurable affairs.

Delicate collarbones jutting out, the only lush thing about her was that mouth. Collagen had nothing on those luscious lips.

She had that million-dollar look that runway models seemed to have. A fragility that, despite her very clever mind, roused a protectiveness in his chest. The last thing she deserved, given the daggers she shot at him. He'd expected her to try to change his mind this morning, *sì*, but not with that brash confidence she exuded just then.

"Come, Ms. Crosetto." He gestured her back toward the limo, taking her wrist in his hand. She was truly delicate in his fingers, and they tightened instinctively. He guided her into the waiting limo and shut the door behind him. Even with the luxurious space, their knees bumped before she tucked them away.

Good, at least one of them needed to be wary of this attraction between them. "You seem to think you have a choice in this situation. My patience runs thin especially as my *nonni* is cooking up a scheme I abhor on the other side of the ocean."

"Your *nonni*?"

"My grandmother."

"I'll make this quick." She swallowed and looked up. "I'm calling your bluff."

He smiled. "You don't have any cards."

She leaned back against the seat, and crossed her legs. Her dress pulled up toward her thighs and he peeked at long, taut muscles. Shamelessly. "I'll not surrender my freedom to a stranger, a stranger moreover with the power and reach that you have, not only in your country but here, to arrange my visa at such short notice, without some security in place. God knows what you'll do to me when—" whatever she saw in his eyes, color darkened her cheeks and she cleared her throat "—what you'll decide for my fate. Even in the worst situations, one always has a choice."

She roused his curiosity so easily and held it. Turned his expectations upside down. So frequently. Unlike any woman he'd ever known. "Why do you think I'll accept any condition of yours?"

"Because you and I are alike. Hungry for new challenges. So full of arrogant belief that we're the best there is. I knew what I was risking when I attacked your security the second time. I knew…and I still couldn't stop. And you…you want to know how I did it. More than you want me in jail. You want to know what other weaknesses there could be in your design. You hate knowing someone better than you exists."

"You're not better than me." He hated that he sounded like a juvenile teenager trying to get one over the smart girl.

She smiled and grooves dug into her cheeks. Her front two teeth were overlapped, a small imperfection that only made her face more distinct, more memorable. More lovely even. Challenge and knowledge simmered in that smile, tugging at his awareness. "Sending me to jail right now doesn't serve your purpose. I'd rot there for who knows how long while what I was capable of doing eats away at you. So I'll let you kidnap me, yes, but at a price."

Laughter punched out of his mouth. *Cristo*, she had guts. And smarts. And a tart mouth he desperately wanted to taste right then. Humor and arousal were an unusual combination but had a languorous effect on his limbs. He ran a hand over his bristly jaw, trying to find the rationality, the reason, beneath both.

If he had any sense, he'd dump her at the nearest police station and wash his hands off.

It was what Leonardo was expecting. What the sane part of him said to do.

But he hadn't arrived at his place in this world without taking risks. By denying his instincts. Forget also the fact that if she went to jail, all her secrets went with her.

He didn't believe for a second that she'd only done it for the challenge. Either it was an impersonal job she took on for money, or someone she knew was deliberately targeting them.

Leonardo and he had worked too hard, for too long, to let some unknown enemy destroy everything they'd built. For now, he'd play along. Plus he'd be no kind of businessman if he didn't use her talents to his benefit. At least in the short term. He'd just have to convince Leo of her usefulness to them.

"Bene," he said.

In the intimacy of the leather interior, her soft gasp pinged on his nerves. Her eyes wide, she stared at him, swallowed, looked away and then back at him again. Her knuckles white against the dark leather.

Cristo, the woman blushed even when she was cornered.

He couldn't help liking the little criminal. He knew what it was to be the weaker one against a stronger, terrifying opponent, to have no way out, the powerlessness that came with it. "State your condition."

"You'll pay me for any services I render, like an outside consultant."

He raised a brow. "You're not bargaining for me to destroy the proof of your crime?"

She shook her head. And he had a feeling it was to hide her expression. "You won't give that up. This way, if I end up in jail, I'll make money to show for it. During the stint, I'll work on proving to you that I have no agenda of my own."

"Making money for hacking my system and then more for fixing it? I was right about you."

"If you were the computer whiz kid the world calls you, you'd have my financials in hand by now."

"Believe me, I was tempted to find the salacious details of your criminal life last night. But my brother reminded me of the importance of doing this through official channels.

"So I ordered a background check on you. Your whole life will be in my hands in a matter of hours," he added, making sure she understood the consequences. "Just because I accept your condition doesn't mean I trust you. Or intend to let you get away with it forever."

Devoid of color, her skin looked alarmingly pale against the black leather. "Is a background check necessary? All you need is to confirm that I'm dirt poor."

He shrugged.

What else was she hiding? And how was he going to explain her presence near him, 24/7, to his family, to the world? The last time he'd been in an actual relationship had been…never. He worked hard, partied hard. For more than a decade, he'd worked sixteen-hour days, buried in his lab. Coming up only for refueling.

Brunetti Cyber Securities came first. Always would.

First because he'd needed to prove to his father that he wasn't the runt he'd been called all his childhood.

And prove himself to Leo even, because he'd been the golden son, the adored Brunetti heir at first. Because Leonardo had been everything Massimo hadn't been able to be.

Later, when Leo had realized the extent of their father's bullying of Massimo, he'd hated Leo's pity, his concern for him. Resented him for thinking Massimo needed handouts, that Massimo was weak. But then success itself had become the motivator; the challenge of building better and better cyber systems had become its own drug.

The more he had, the more he'd wanted. The more he wanted his father and his family and his brother to be beholden to his company for fueling much needed funds into Brunetti Finances.

Suddenly, the answer came to him. Two problems and one solution. A tangible use of the attraction between them. An explanation for her presence with him, night and day.

He'd get her to trust him with the complete truth, then he might even take her to bed. Scratch the itch out of his system. Her innocent act would have to drop when he had the background check in his hands.

He pulled up his phone and texted his assistant waiting outside to ready a contract with all the required confidentiality clauses. Another text to notify Leo about the slight modification to his plans. "You'll have the contract by the time we land. Under one—"

"I won't leave without it."

He shook his head. "Not even I can come up with a

contract like that immediately. Not without having that background check in hand first."

"How do I know I can trust you?"

"You don't." He shrugged. The hiss of her breath, the filthy curse reverberating in the confined space, made his mouth twitch.

He was enjoying this—this pitting his will against hers, this anticipation in his gut as he waited to see what she'd do next. More than he enjoyed anything with a woman in a long time. Even more than sex. He frowned at the runaway thought. "I have a countercondition of my own."

"You're already blackmailing me, kidnapping me, threatening me with incarceration. What else is there?"

"You'll be my partner for the duration. I'll compensate you for that, too."

"Partner? What kind of a partner?" Color left her cheeks, her eyes searching his. "For the last time, Mr. Brunetti, I'm not for sale. I'm not what you think—"

"Calm down, Natalie," he interrupted her, trying her name on his tongue and liking it. Her eyes sought his in the relative dark, awareness shining through them. She hadn't missed the intimacy of it, either. "It's just another part of our deal, *sì*?"

"Explain. Now, please."

"I have to explain your presence at my side, 24/7. I need a romantic partner for the foreseeable future. This way—"

"You've lost your mind. I'm not staying in Italy any longer than I have to. And I refuse to be your... Why the hell would a man like you need a pretend girlfriend?"

"A man like me?"

He grinned. She glared. "You're supersmart, obviously given you're one of the tech billionaires under thirty in the world. You're—" she licked her lips then and he waited with arrested breath "—a walking, talking stud muffin. Not counting all that dynasty crap you threw at me. Why—?"

"What does a woman do with a stud muffin?"

She rolled her eyes and he laughed. "Why do you need a pretend girlfriend?"

"I was thinking a pretend fiancée actually." Her eyes bugged and he grinned, explaining, "An ex-girlfriend that I can't shake off and my *nonni* have joined forces. Believe me, it's enough to scare a grown man."

"So you don't want to hurt their feelings?"

This time, when he laughed, it felt as if his chest would burst open. The minx was such a contrasting mix of street savvy and naïveté, of smarts and innocence. She'd make a hell of a distraction from the lethargy that had filled him of late when it came to women.

"Feelings, of any of the parties involved, are the least of my concern. Greta, my *nonni*, is extremely stubborn, and has antiquated views about the whole dynasty and its continuation and legacy and all that rot. For some unfathomable reason, apparently, she's decided that Gisela Fiore, who comes with a fortune of her own, would be a sweet, biddable wife for me. Gisela is a mistake I shouldn't have indulged in, and has been…problematic since I ended our purely physical relationship almost six months ago."

For all her sass, color skimmed up Natalie's cheeks. "Problematic how?"

"She knows my relationship patterns. She knew it was only an affair. When I retreated to my lab—refueled and ready—"

"What do you mean...refueled?"

"After every big project release, I need to fill the well, so to speak."

"And you do this...*refueling* by sleeping with a woman you don't care about?"

Her distaste made him frown. "I care about the woman's pleasure. And mine. But, *sì*. Gisela knew that. Knew my pattern. I made it clear. After it was over, she started texting me a hundred times a day. She'd cry, make a scene at the few social events I attended. She flew to San Francisco and accosted me at a cyber security conference.

"Showed up outside our estate in Lake Como. Cornered my brother, Leo, at one of the events where her father was present, too."

"And her father is someone whose feelings you do give a damn about?" she said tartly.

Massimo scowled. "Giuseppe Fiore is one of the most powerful banking tycoons in Milan, in all of Italy. BCS is in the running for a hundred-billion-euro security contract with his banks that spans a decade. Leo thinks it's going to make dealing with him awkward because of Gisela.

"Why should a fling she came into with her eyes open cause problems for me now?"

"Because people are not algorithms that give you the same, expected results every time?"

"Once Giuseppe sees me with you, he'll understand that Gisela and I are long over. And this is the best way for me to keep an eye on you."

"If this tycoon's so rich and powerful, and his daughter's good enough to be your...*whatever*, why not just marry her? Or are you holding out for love?"

He stared at her, wondering if she was joking again. Steady brown eyes held his. "Tut, tut, Natalie...you disappoint me. The last thing I need in my life is a wife who wants love and all the rainbows it brings with it. I have nothing to give a wife at present. Or in the foreseeable future.

"Just do your part, *si*? The compensation I provide should be big enough for you to get over your distaste for me," he mocked.

Her nostrils flared. "And if I say no? If I tell your ex and your grandmother that it's all a big pretense?"

"You won't do that."

"I just—"

"Be smart about this, Natalie." All humor fled his tone. "If I find you've told me the truth about your financials, about this not being a job, then what do you have to lose? For once in your life, maybe you could use your interesting capabilities to make a living. Spend a few months in the lap of luxury in Milan. Pretend to be the fiancée of the most—"

"Arrogant, high-handed man on the planet?"

"So?"

"Fine. I agree to your conditions."

"Bene."

He stepped out of the limo and helped her do the same, keeping his fingers around her wrist. He liked having the feel of her in his hands, this mystery hacker who'd haunted his days and nights for weeks.

"All that's left now is to swap our life histories and practice the intimacy we have to pretend in front of my family and the whole world."

A pithy curse fell from her mouth and Massimo looked down at her.

She was truly the most interesting woman he'd ever met. He wouldn't hesitate to send her to jail if he found her loyalties lay with their enemy, but he would regret it all the same.

And he didn't understand even that negligible emotion dogging his rationality, his judgment.

It had never done so before.

CHAPTER FOUR

AFTER A TRANSATLANTIC flight to Milan with a creative genius who peppered her with a million incisive questions meant to unsettle her lies. Throwing in a magnificent view of white-tipped Alps, which she'd probably never see again in her life—except maybe on the return flight on her way to jail in New York. Then a quick helicopter ride up to the shores of Lake Como—because, of course, the once-in-a-lifetime scenic drive from Milan to the lake would take forever and time was a precious commodity to a tech billionaire. Finally arriving at a destination where she was nothing but a prisoner, Natalie foolishly assumed she would become oblivious to her surroundings—not the man, of course—or at least be too exhausted mentally and physically to take much more in.

She was wrong.

The chopper landed on the side of a hill, in a sea of lush, perfectly manicured gardens with azaleas and gigantic rhododendrons and a long avenue of tall plane trees that created a walkway to the lakefront. A small boat floated at the end of the steps. Beyond, the calm waters of Lake Como glittered like a dark blanket creating a stunning sight littered with boats of various sizes floating lazily to the gorgeously lit-up houses and villages scattered about.

As Natalie followed Massimo, who seemed to have forgotten about her existence, amid carefully sculpted flower beds, she spotted a hidden cave enclosed by more azaleas and even an artificial Japanese-style pond.

"Your family owns this villa?" she said, her breath catching in her throat.

Massimo stopped, took a look around absentmindedly and then turned to her. "*Sì*. One of the Brunettis, a count or a duke, maybe, I think in the nineteenth century, took possession of a Benedictine monastery in these grounds and converted it into a sumptuous noble residence. It's been in the family's possession ever since. Greta will cram a history lesson down your throat if she catches you staring at it like that."

Even his mockery couldn't fracture the awe in her chest. Fountains with water glittering out like liquid gold because of strategically placed lights, a gazebo with creepers enveloping it, two statues of majestic lions at the sides of the carriage entrance… How could he sound so dismissive and unaffected by his family's legacy? "I've never seen such beautiful gardens."

"You'd love it in spring when they're a riot of color. They're Leonardo's pride. He personally tends to them along with a team of gardeners. He can make the most reluctant plant blossom. He…loves the land and the villa and the…legacy of it all."

She was out of breath as they walked up the small,

steep path while he simply marched on. "You don't?" she asked, something in his tone snagging her attention.

"I like being the one who saved it, the one who held it for the Brunettis so that they could show it off for another century," he added mysteriously.

She frowned, wondering at the contradictions of the man.

Finally, they came around the bend to a square plot that housed the villa itself. A grand entrance portico with wide stairs that sloped toward the lake straddled the villa, which would offer three-sixty-degree views of the lake and the mountains from the grand terrace even now overflowing with guests.

The white stucco facade gleamed under the light thrown from the lake. Nat sucked in a breath as the sounds of music and people chatting in Italian flowed over her skin. A line of luxury cars stood like gatekeepers, tasked with keeping riffraff, like her, out.

She shivered even though the wind coming off the lake was more balmy than cold. Cicadas whispered all around them, the scents from the orangery they'd walked by thick and pungent in the air.

It was a world away from Brooklyn and her cheap studio apartment, a world away from everything she'd ever known.

Through the high arched front entrance, she could see suave men dressed in black suits and refined women dressed in cocktail finery with diamonds glittering at their throats and wrists. Uniformed waiters passing around champagne flutes so fine that Nat wondered if they'd break at the slightest pressure.

She rubbed her sweating palms on her hips, which only brought her attention to her own outfit. A thread of shame filled her chest and she chased it away with much needed anger. God, she'd worked hard for every small thing she owned. To make an honest living for herself and for Frankie.

She felt the heat of Massimo's body next to her, before she heard the curse from his mouth. Frowning, she craned her neck to see him. Flashes of light revealed the tension in his brow, that perfectly carved jaw so tight that it almost seemed fragile. If she didn't know better, she'd have thought he was no more inclined to go in than she was.

The suavely sophisticated man who'd taunted her was nowhere to be seen. In his place was a stranger with tension thrumming tightly through his lean frame.

"Massimo?" she whispered, unable to stem the concern she heard in her voice. "Is something wrong?"

"My father is here," he answered softly, before he blew out another soft curse and shook his head. "He is a bully of the worst kind."

"Must run in the family, then," she quipped.

"No." His soft denial was emphatic enough that her head jerked to him. Glittering gray eyes held hers. "I'm nothing like my father." He rubbed his jaw, a tell she was beginning to recognize he did when stressed. "*Dios mio*, I forgot it's his birthday week. That means Greta checks him out of the rehabilitation clinic and parades him in front of our family and friends in an annual tradition. That means—" his gaze swung to the luxury vehicles "—everyone is here."

"Your father lives at a clinic?" She'd gotten the sense from him that family was important to him. Yet, he stared at his family's villa like it was a nest of vipers.

"He's a recovering alcoholic. The recovery, if we can call it that, has been in progress for a decade now. Leonardo put him there years ago. My brother…he's the best at eliminating anything that could damage our name, our business. Our legacy."

The bitterness in his words was unmistakable. "What do you mean your grandmother parades him?"

"You didn't get the sordid Brunetti history online before you attacked BCS?"

The man changed skins as easily as a chameleon— one minute a charming rogue, the next a cunning businessman determined to make her spill her secrets against her own best interests. "I told you, I knew nothing about who and what you are."

Hesitation flickered in his eyes, before he cast another glance toward the villa. "If you're to be exposed to them… My father, for most of my childhood, went on alcohol-fueled rampages. He embezzled funds from the company account for his personal use. Affairs with numerous women—both willing and unwilling—lavish parties at the villa… Think of it as a decades-long, out-of-control party that Greta turned away from.

"By the time his misuse of company funds and resources came to Leonardo's notice, Brunetti Finances, which had once been the leading finance giant in all of Italy, had been on the verge of bankruptcy. A dynasty reduced to nothing but a deck of cards standing on quicksand.

"Leo had to use every inch of his business acumen to stop it from crumbling around our ears. He slogged night and day to get us out from under debt, took control of the board. I designed an e-commerce tool at the same time. He brought in millions in investors, persuaded me to build and release it myself instead of selling the design like I had planned to. I created Brunetti Cyber Securities under the family company's umbrella and launched the tool. With the revenue from it, we stopped Brunetti Finances from going under.

"Silvio, kicking and screaming, was checked into rehab. My father's still a powerful man—so many of the investors Leo brought in are of his generation. So… lest the world think we're any less than the grand dynasty we're supposed to be, lest they wonder we're not all one big happy family, we parade him annually and pretend to be his adoring sons."

Natalie refused to let the stringent quality of his words, something that almost sounded like pain, touch her.

Massimo Brunetti had blackmailed her. He was a ruthless bastard who thought women were for refueling his… He was the scion of a powerful if *dysfunctional* dynasty; he wouldn't have even noticed her if she'd fallen at his feet. There was no need to see him as anything but a two-dimensional enemy.

No need to feel this…answering emotion in her chest, this urge to touch him and smooth out his brow.

Nope, nope, nope. So not going there.

She tugged his wrist. "We don't have to go in, then. It's not as if you can't go against their wishes, is it? I mean, you're a grown man. You run your own company. Who cares if—"

His laughter cut through her persuasive tirade, sending shock waves through her body. The warm, masculine sounds reached through her skin, into her chest, enveloping her. Burrowing inside of her.

She turned to look at him and it got worse. Much worse.

Moonlight bathed his perfect bone structure, caressing the high planes of his forehead and cheekbones, lavishing that lush mouth with tender care. His nostrils flared, grooves digging around his mouth.

She tried to ignore the attention his laughter had drawn toward them. A shiver went through her as she felt more than one set of eyes watching her, watching them from the lounge and from the terrace above. "What?" she said, channeling sarcasm.

The flash of his white smile in the darkness sent awareness through her. It wasn't fair that one man could be that gorgeous.

"You sounded as though you were championing me. Is it possible I'm growing on you, *cara mia*?"

The endearment threw her even more off balance. "As much as a malware bot could grow on an encrypted system," she threw at him. "Seriously, Massimo, can we leave?" she implored.

This time, his smile reached his gray eyes, deepening them into molten pools of warmth. "It would only be postponing the drama. With Greta, it's better to get it done as soon as possible. All you have to do is bat your eyelashes, pretend to adore me and thank the guests when they tell you what a lucky woman you are."

"At what time during our short and forced acquaintance did I give the impression that I'm of the kind to bat my eyelashes and adore a man for simply existing?"

He reached for her, his large hands encompassing her in warmth. "What worries you so much, anyway?"

"I'm not worried. I…"

His gaze held hers, searching, studying. "Natalie…"

"No one's going to believe you, Massimo."

"Believe what?"

"That I'm your fiancée. That you could fall for me. I don't—" she moved her arm to encompass the sheer elegance of everything surrounding them "—belong in this world."

His gaze raked over her, from her wavy, curly hair—even more uncontrollable after the flight—to her off-shoulder sweater, which instead of looking stylish, to her just felt tacky in this environment, to the scuff marks on her secondhand leather boots. "*No*, you don't."

No way was she going to let him see the ridiculous dismay settling like a boulder in her throat. What the hell was wrong with her? "We finally agree on something."

"They'll believe exactly because of that," he said cryptically. "It's too late, anyway. Even she's here."

"She who?"

He turned completely toward her and ate up the little distance separating them. When he raised his hand to her face, every inch of her froze. Her mouth felt dry, her pulse racing through her.

"She who I need to send a message to in the most diplomatic way possible." Gray gaze holding hers, he paused an inch away from her face. "I'm going to touch you, *cara mia—sì?*"

"Not *sì,* Massimo," she said, panic brewing in her belly, and his mouth twitched. "Why do you want to touch me?"

"For the audience," he said, his eyes saying something else completely. "I'm going to touch you and kiss you, and maybe… All you have to do is close your eyes and think of your future, unmarred by visits to jail cells."

"You're a rogue and twisted to get your kicks from a woman you're blackmailing."

Instead of anger, his eyes glittered with warmth and desire. "Shall I tell you the bare truth, then, *bella mia?* The one small nugget that distracts me when I should be focused on a hundred other priorities?"

It took everything she had to not give in to the urge to lean into him. Already, the scent of him—cologne, sweat and the cigar she'd seen him smoking this morning—entrenched deep under her skin. "What?"

"It's for the audience, *sì.* But also, for me. For us. I should very much like to learn what you taste like, Natalie, and every time you lick your lower lip, which you do, any time I set my eyes on that mouth, it's like you're inviting me to do the same. Every time you devour me with those big eyes, my nose, my mouth, my hair…you're—"

Warmth unlike she'd ever experienced uncurled low in her belly, spreading its wicked fingers to each limb until she was made of honey. He'd barely even touched her and she was branded by the honesty in his words.

Desire pervaded his every word, his accent deepening with each breath. "I'm not, I mean… I wasn't…"

Something almost like possessiveness flitted in his eyes. Because, really, what did she know of men. Especially of men like Massimo Brunetti. "One kiss, Natalie. Be honest. Tell me you haven't wondered, too. Tell me you haven't been thinking of the heat between us and I'll make do with a kiss on the cheek."

She simply nodded, no words coming to her aid. A light-headedness traversed through her entire body, stealing her good sense.

If he'd coerced her, if he'd grabbed her hands or pulled her to him roughly, the spell of the moment would have broken. If he had taken it as his due, instead of asking, the tentative connection between them would've fractured. She would've regained the little common sense she possessed.

But he didn't.

Massimo didn't do anything that she expected of him. And when he did the unexpected, he stole away the ground from under her.

As if she were the most precious possession to come into his hands, his fingers landed on her wrists softly. Turning one, he raised it to his mouth. The first press of his lips against the sensitive skin sent tremors of longing through her. He didn't let her look away, either. The flick of his tongue over the plump vein, the stubble surrounding his mouth scraping in contrast, the sight of his arrogant head bent to her wrist…everything conspired and coalesced into a temptation neither her body nor her mind could resist.

Knees trembling, she let out a soft gasp, an erotic sound that deepened the gray fire in his eyes. When he pulled her toward him, she went, desperately needing more. And he delivered, his fingers digging into her shoulders, moving lower, touching every inch of her. The first, barely there slide of her breasts against his chest was a sensation she'd remember forever. Breath punched out of her on a long hiss, the strength of his powerful thighs a teasing caress against her own.

He let his fingers splay on her back. The tips reached the dip of her waist, spanned it and then moved back up. The rough hitch of his breath was music to her ears, bringing the knowledge to her ensnared senses that he wanted her just as much as she did him. When he moved his hands up from her waist, just a couple of tempting inches, the tips barely even grazing the sides of her breasts, she stiffened, tried to move away and stumbled until her hip bumped against his front and her thigh was caught between his.

Electricity zinged through her veins. He was so solidly masculine around her, both a haven of warmth and demanding need. Fingers on her shoulders held her rigid as he bent that mouth finally. A kiss from that mouth at her cheek, at her temple, the tip of her nose—like wings of a butterfly. And then he brushed his mouth against hers. "From the moment I realized you were the hacker who'd haunted my days and nights…all I could think of was doing this."

Nat jerked in his embrace, the sensations generated by the contact so delicious. So hot. If not for the heat in her veins, she'd have laughed for he did it with that scientific precision, as if an inch of her couldn't be left unexplored. Tired of waiting for him, she followed his lips with her own, seeking the heat and promise.

Sensations jerked through her at the hard contact. She licked his lower lip, pressed herself into his warmth.

She heard the soft curse he left on her lips, saw shock and something indefinable widen his eyes. As if he, too, had been unprepared for the spark to turn into a full-blown fire. And then he was repeating the torment all over again. For a hard, lean man, he had the most incredibly soft lips. And his beard, oh, it was such a contrasting scrape against the softness of his kisses, a pleading moan pushed out of her own mouth.

"You taste sweet and tart, *cara mia*," he said huskily, as lost as she was.

Kissing her all over, his long fingers climbing up her back, sliding around the nape of her neck, sneaking into her hair. And then, suddenly, his grip tightened there. When he pulled, her face tilted back, an offering she willingly gave.

Desire stamped out everything else from his arrogant features—the casual humor, the ambitious billionaire—leaving a starkness to him.

Gaze locked on her own, this time, when he bent that mouth to hers, there was no exploration. No entreating. He nipped at her lower lip, and blew warm breath over the hurt. Licked and plundered. A continuous assault that made tingles spread out. He took, and yet gave, such indescribable pleasure. The stroke of his tongue was a caress that had her gasping into his mouth. He licked into hers with an erotic hunger that had her rising up to her toes, burrowing into him to get even closer, clinging to his solid shoulders with shallow breaths. The scent of him, so familiarly male already, coated every inch of her.

Her own hands wandered restlessly, from the scrape of his beard to his neck and into his hair, pulling, tugging, wanting more of him. Desperate to keep the madness going. She moved them over his chest, loving the sinew, thanking the stars that he'd taken off the jacket. His shirt was no barrier against the heat he radiated. Air was something he granted her amid the hungry kisses.

"*Altro*, Natalie *mia*. I need more." His heated whisper inflamed her with its honesty. The differences between them melted away under the heat of their touch.

Tongues dueled, teeth banged, as the kiss lost its finesse and became nothing but hunger. A gateway to something much more.

Her back was bowed, his hands at her waist pulling her up, his fingers digging painfully into her hips. Her breasts crushed against his chest. Natalie could do nothing but drown in the avalanche of sensations. Revel in the pleasure coursing through her.

With a growly moan, Natalie pushed away at his hands, and thrust her hips into his. Driven by instinct, desperate for more. Not wanting the moment to end.

The slight graze of his erection against her soft belly before he pushed her firmly back jolted her out of the feral need pumping through her veins. His curse was loud and harsh in the slumbering silence of the night all around them.

She stared into the piercing gaze, stunned, mouth

stinging. His breath was harsher than her own, his pupils dilated. The lean chest falling and rising in a rhythm her own matched. Her hands fell away from him, empty. Slowly, softly, their surroundings—the air redolent with the scent of flowers, their audience, more than one set of eyes devouring them—began to filter through her consciousness. Yet, nothing could penetrate fully the haze of pleasure the kiss had left in her mind. Her limbs, her belly, her breasts…she felt like she was swimming in honey. Naked.

"That went farther than I anticipated." He spoke slowly, as if each word had to be pulled out. Hoarse. His English thickly accented for the first time. "To go any further, *cara mia*, we'll have to revisit our—"

"I'm not sleeping with you," Nat somehow managed to whisper, her pulse still zigzagging all over the place. Desperate to cut off whatever asinine, calculating announcement he'd have made. It was bad enough she had crawled all over him, in front of his family and friends, no less. Had lost herself in that kiss, completely.

She couldn't let him insult her, too, by offering to pay for more services rendered or some such.

The kiss and the intensity of it had thrown him, too. As inexperienced as she was with arrogant, confounding who kissed like fantasies given life, she could see the contradiction in his eyes, the tension in his brow. He'd expected it to be a pleasant diversion, for both himself and his bloody audience, a game of kissing the criminal, but it had slipped out of his control and morphed into something much more.

But for her, it had been her first kiss. A memory to be cherished.

For once in her life, she'd been allowed to be self-ish. Given the sex-god incarnate staring at her, she was allowed to be foolish and flighty. Once. But no more.

"Why not?" he taunted back.

"Now you sound like that pretty, rich boy denied his new toy."

Color flooded his cheeks. "You can't deny the connection between us. From that first moment. It's already messing with my rationality."

She fisted her hands at her sides. Better than running them over her trembling lips. "Because we're not equals, Mr. Brunetti." He scowled at her use of his formal name. "How can I be sure what your motives are? How would I know if you're doing it because you want to try the novelty of having the hacker who bested you catering to your desires, under your control, in your bed—" she purposely made her words crude, for her own benefit "—or because you're arrogant enough to believe that you're such a good lay that I'll spill all my secrets to you in gratitude?"

He tilted her chin up, mouth tensed. "I know my own mind, *cara mia*. I want you, Natalie." His gaze touched her lips with such possessiveness that contradicted the logical, rational man she glimpsed in him. "I've never been attracted to a woman so much that I want to own both her body and mind."

His jaw tightened, the raw honesty of his words a revelation to both of them.

She wanted to believe him so desperately. Wished

she had that innocence, those rose-tinted glasses she'd lost so long ago, to see all of this as some fantastic fairy tale. That all of it could have a happy ending.

Even for a short affair where she could live, be herself for a small capsule of time. But she wasn't built to have casual, torrid affairs with complex men.

"It doesn't have to complicate matters."

"Could you be so arrogant to think I'll fall at your feet?"

"Arrogance has nothing to do with it. That kiss speaks for itself."

"You've turned my world upside down in the matter of a few hours. You hold my fate in your hands.

"If I sleep with you, can you ever be sure if I was doing it because I wanted to persuade you to let me go or because I really wanted to have sex with you?" She wiped the taste of him from her mouth, feeling a sudden dejection. "All the power is in your hands, Massimo. Which means neither of us could ever be sure of our motives."

He didn't quite flinch. A vein jumped in his temple, and he sighed. "Even having been on the other side once, power and privilege are still hard to separate from yourself."

Just like that, he shredded all the defenses she'd propped up against him into mere dust. She'd have been less scared if he'd been less understanding, less kind, less... *Massimo*.

No man, she had a feeling, was close to the complexity of Massimo Brunetti.

And if he grew up amid this, how could he know what it meant to be powerless?

He took her hand in his and laced their fingers. When she shivered, he pulled her to his side with an arm around her shoulders. Even fighting it, Natalie couldn't help leaning on him, stealing his warmth for herself.

When he propelled her forward, she went, like a puppet whose strings he held with those elegant fingers.

The logic she'd sprouted sounded so right.

Now if only she could get her body to stop fixating on the taste and warmth of Massimo's kiss and treat this whole thing…as a job. A job on which her entire future depended.

CHAPTER FIVE

THE THEME OF elegant affluence continued indoors including the wide steps and the portico. More fool her if she expected anything less. Even the remnants of his kiss couldn't numb her to the decadent elegance of his home.

The large marble foyer had a wraparound marble staircase with beautifully dressed men and women drifting around it. A large Venetian chandelier hung from the high ceiling with hand-painted frescoes that she had to crane her neck to look at. Her entire apartment could fit into the front lounge. A dark red Persian rug covered a small area and beautiful, original works of art hung on the wall.

Natalie could feel so many sets of eyes on her and Massimo and soft whispers across the room as if the cicadas had drifted inside. She was suddenly glad Massimo had vetoed her request to leave. Prolonging this moment wouldn't change the reality of who she was.

A large, rectangular, gold-edged mirror hung on one cream wall. One passing glance at it as Massimo tugged her with him told Natalie she stood out like a sore thumb in this crowd. She grabbed a champagne flute from a uniformed waiter and threw it back as if it were cheap, boxed wine.

Massimo cast her a wry look. "You're not getting drunk on me, *cara mia*."

"Why not? It's not as if I can contribute anything important to the conversation around me."

He rubbed a finger over a drop lingering on her upper lip. The heat from the pad of his thumb tingled her skin. "Maybe not to them, *si*? But to me, you're the most interesting person in this room." A lock of hair fell forward onto his forehead as he leaned down to whisper. His eyes shone with a roguish glint, his mouth tilting up on one side. "Take pity on me, *bella mia*. Only you here with me is making this evening bearable."

Her pulse raced. The villa, the grounds, nothing could equal the effortless magic he weaved with his words. "You're even more dangerous when you set out to be charming." She pushed the lock of hair away from his face, and then snatched her hand back when he leaned into her touch. How could his face, his body, his expressions, feel so familiar already to her? Granted, it was hard to maintain animosity toward a man who kissed like it was the single most fascinating experience of his life. "You want me to believe you're not part of this crowd?"

"I was the stereotypical geek growing up. Socially awkward, sick far too often, hiding behind the escape that computers provided. Trying to persuade myself that I didn't need my father's or this crowd's approval."

She could do nothing but stare.

My father is a bully. Suddenly, his words, the tension in him before coming in, made all the sense.

"Ah... I've rendered you mute with my sad story, *sì?*"

She shook her head, something she'd long buried searching for voice now. Longing to be shared with a man who was from a different world and yet, somehow, she knew would understand. "The loneliness was the hardest for me. For all their rationality, computers don't offer warmth. Or a kind word, when needed."

His jaw tight, his eyes searched hers. "Now you pity me."

She grabbed his hand and pulled him to her. The stubble on his jaw pricked her palm, his sharp breaths stroked her skin, and still she couldn't pull away. Couldn't get her heart to disengage. "I'm just having difficulty imagining this...hot, sexy, gorgeous man in front of me as an awkward, pimply, pasty geek."

"I never said pimply or pasty," he said, before he took her mouth in a savage kiss that knocked the breath out of her very lungs. The searing press of their lips lasted maybe a few seconds and yet it was hot, all-consuming, a synergy of more than just their mouths.

Hands on her shoulders, he pushed her back too soon. His eyes mesmerized with the heat in them. "If I apologize for that, I will not mean it."

She licked her lip, wanting to savor the lingering taste of him. "I...just..."

He grinned and she grinned back like a fool.

If nothing else, the fast and hard kiss made Natalie numb to every other dynamic and drama that played out over the next few hours. Numbed her toward the glittering butterflies sipping champagne ever so delicately and the men fawning over them.

Only her *bitchery* felt more than justified as she met an awful number of perfectly horrid people who stared at her as if she were an exhibit.

"Ooh, look at the low-class, unrefined American in her thrift-store clothes and shoes, pretending to belong on one of Milan's most wanted bachelors' arm," she whispered, sick of that feeling in her belly.

"You didn't tell me you speak Italian so well," he said, confirming her understanding of the looks cast her way. A pinprick of hurt flashed and she shrugged it away.

"I don't have to speak Italian. Elitist snobbery, apparently, transcends the boundaries of language."

His laughter was raucous, booming, shaking his body, translating the motion to her own as she was neatly wedged against his side. He looked breathtakingly gorgeous. Conversations around them came to a stunning halt, the silence left behind so loud that Natalie gazed around with wide eyes.

"You know what I like about you the most, *cara mia*?"

The stupid organ that was her heart went pitter-patter. "That I'm far cleverer than you are?"

His teeth flashed at her and she had the overwhelming urge to taste that smile again. To take the warmth of it into her. "That tart mouth and what comes out of it…" His voice dipped, turned huskier, his gaze riveted to her mouth. "How is it possible that it also tastes so incredibly sweet?"

Her cheeks heated. "Massimo, please don't—"

"How much longer must I wait before you introduce your latest toy to us, Massimo?"

This had to be Greta. Natalie cringed at having been caught staring at Massimo like a lovesick fool.

The older woman, clad in a white-and-black cocktail dress that went superbly well with her gray hair, speared her with a frosty look that made her disapproval apparent without words.

Massimo dutifully bent his cheek for his grandmother's kiss.

"Nonni, this is my fiancée, Natalie Crosetto—" the lie flowed smoothly from his lips "—the most interesting woman I've met in…forever—" turned into a truth that knocked the breath out of her lungs in the next second. He lifted their laced fingers to his mouth and pressed a kiss to the back of her hand. "She let me… *persuade* her to marry me."

He winked at her as she shook Greta's hand, answering her invasive questions about her life. About her family. About her past. For a wicked moment, she played with telling the woman all the details of her colorful past. But she had no wish to embarrass Massimo or herself. She nodded like a dutiful child while Greta, with a voice that sounded like a boom box and with heavily accented English, told her what a privilege it was to land the scion of the Brunetti clan.

Natalie had had enough when Greta started rattling on and on about pedigree. "Is your grandson a fish to be caught, Mrs. Giovanni?" she said, tongue-in-cheek.

"You would offend your relationship with Giuseppe

Fiore for this nobody, Massimo?" Greta said, loudly enough for everyone to hear her. "Reject an heiress like Gisela, who would make you the perfect bride?"

"I offer insult to no one, Nonni," Massimo replied in an equally steely tone, before he tucked Natalie into his side protectively. The smile bestowed on Natalie was warm, his embrace too honest and too possessive. So dangerous that even she wanted to buy in to their pretense.

He placed another kiss on the underside of her wrist.

Natalie shivered, struggling against falling into his spell again. Neither did she miss the presence of the petite woman, her voluptuous curves dressed in a green silk that was the height of sophistication, her pretty face artfully made up to accentuate the dark black eyes and the scarlet painted mouth, hanging a few steps back, listening to their conversation as if her life depended on it.

"I fell in love with a woman with whom I have a world of things in common," Massimo said in a husky voice, his eyes holding hers. "She's nothing like anyone I've ever met. Even I didn't expect it. Giuseppe or you or any other person has nothing to do with this."

With that he pivoted them away in another direction without waiting for Greta's reply.

Nat swallowed the thanks that rose to her lips. She was damned if she was going to thank him for rescuing her from a situation he'd put her in in the first place. She managed to flit through the guests at his side for the next two hours without running away screaming.

All through it, Nat was aware of the tall, dark, striking man who watched her every move like a hawk.

Leonardo Brunetti, the only other person there who knew what she was. The cold hauteur in his eyes, the distaste in his expression as he noted Massimo's arm around her waist, said more than enough.

Massimo seemed to be saving the best for last, *yippee*. "Silence and the four walls of a jail cell don't sound like such a bad prospect right now," she said as he pulled her in yet another direction. "What do you think is the market rate for enduring emotional trauma these days?"

Massimo smiled down at her. She tried to ignore that it lit up his whole face. The reassurance in the way he squeezed her fingers. Devil or angel, she didn't know what to make of this man. "Ahh…but I would miss you, *cara mia*." She stiffened when he tugged her tight against him, his mouth buried at her temple. "Don't let Leonardo scare you, *sì*? My brother's bark is much worse than his bite."

Natalie nodded, not at all surprised that he'd noted her reaction to his older brother. He was far too perceptive. Barely two days since they'd met and he'd already tripped her up far too many times.

The only person who would actually meet her eyes, despite the confusion in her own when Massimo introduced her, was his grandmother's stepdaughter, Alessandra Giovanni. Who turned out to be *the famous supermodel* Alessandra Giovanni, naturally. Almost six feet tall, the woman had a stunning face that photographers over the world loved, with a bombshell body that would fire any red-blooded man's fantasy. *And* she'd grown up with Massimo and Leonardo after coming to live with Greta and her father when she'd been twelve.

Any twinge of jealousy Natalie was foolish enough to feel that this gorgeous creature knew Massimo intimately died at the genuine affection in her smile. "Love and you, Massimo? Has the world turned upside down?" she said in an American accent that warmed Nat.

"She's a hacker who can take down the best security systems in the world," Massimo whispered in outraged mockery that made Nat roll her eyes. "She took me down, Alex. Me!"

"Ah…" Alessandra said, her twinkling gaze studying them both. "Now that makes perfect sense." Then the woman colored. "Not that you're not lovely enough for Massimo to want beyond that. You're just…so not his type." She grimaced and covered her face with a groan. Natalie liked her a lot for that imperfection. "I'm making an utter ass of myself, aren't I? What I mean is you have to be extraordinarily special for Massimo to have not only fallen in love with you so quickly but to have even considered forever… Nothing, and I mean nothing, comes before his tech empire for Massimo."

"Let's just say Massimo couldn't bear it that I might be better than him," Nat replied. "And in a strategy of if you can't beat them join them, he locked me down in a contract I couldn't resist."

Alessandra laughed at that. A lovely, genuine smile that was like a beacon of light amid the artificial glitter around them. "Oh, I like you, Natalie. Please feel free to come to me if you need ammunition against him."

Her smile dimming, Natalie nodded. She would've loved to have a friend like Alessandra for real. But this wasn't her life. This incredibly sophisticated woman wouldn't say hello to Natalie if she knew all the things she'd done to survive.

None of these people would, even Massimo.

This was a virtual reality program she was projecting herself into.

By the time they reached the two gentlemen—she used that word for lack of a better term, for they both studied her from top to toe with an invasive and at the same time dismissive curiosity that raised all her hackles—Massimo had saved for the last, Nat couldn't give a damn.

Leonardo Brunetti, like Massimo, dominated the space he occupied. Like his brother, he was lean but broad-shouldered, his face more rugged and brutish than sharp like Massimo's, cynicism and disdain all but set into the planes. An aura of power clung to him like a second skin. Unlike Massimo, who she'd realized possessed a devilish sense of humor, there was nothing gentle or merciful about the curve of his mouth or the icy blue gaze he leveled at her.

Here was a man who was determined to be pleased by nothing and no one. At least, not just her.

The second man, Silvio, was as tall as his sons and a mixture of both. Hair gray at the temples, his face only retained a vestige of the handsome youth he must have been. His features seemed as if they'd been smudged and distorted by years of alcohol. Puffy bags sagged under his eyes while his mouth seemed to be curled into a permanent sneer.

Next to his powerful, dominating sons, he was a pale imitation, in both stature and presence. And yet, having been a recipient of it far too many times, Natalie could see the casual cruelty he was capable of in his rough features, in the sneer he directed at her, could imagine him as a rough brute bullying a young, innocent boy.

Massimo's arm around her waist tightened. Nat leaned into his weight, seeking and giving comfort automatically. As if they were together against the whole world. Not that he noticed. He was too caught up in whatever mind game ensued between his father and him.

"Massimo?" She nudged him, needing for the long day to be over.

"Natalie, this is my father, Silvio Brunetti, and my brother, Leonardo. This is Natalie Crosetto, my fiancée."

"What do you do, Ms. Crosetto?" Silvio shot at her without a preamble, his gaze utterly dismissive of her attire.

"I'm a clerk at a loan office, Mr. Brunetti," Natalie answered, refusing to let another snotty man make her feel ashamed.

"Your family—"

"My family is no one, since my father walked out one night and left me to fend for myself. If not for a conscientious social worker, I wouldn't have known he had fathered a son with a different woman who he also abandoned."

She felt Massimo's surprise at her side, his frown.

It wasn't as if he wasn't going to find out soon, anyway. And really, having met his snotty family, she felt as if she had nothing to be ashamed of. Even her deadbeat dad.

"Ah…at least you've saved us the bother of a background check," Silvio finished simply.

Natalie couldn't even muster outrage. Massimo could be called Prince Charming if this was the role model he'd grown up with.

His gaze swung to Massimo's. "You should be careful, Massimo, or you'll lose more than Giuseppe's contract. Empires are not built on weaknesses." Something oily smirked from his eyes. "You do not need to marry the girl to enjoy her."

"I don't need your advice," Massimo ground out through gritted teeth. Fury cast a dark shadow on his features. "On empires or weaknesses. Or how to treat women for that matter, *sì*?"

"You were always the weak link in our family," Silvio said, a cruel sneer to his mouth that disturbed her on so many levels.

Was this what Massimo had had to put up with, growing up?

Silvio bent toward Massimo. "Leo tells me the security system you've built has been breached. I knew you shouldn't be trusted, not in the long term. I warned your brother to not tie Brunetti Finances with you. Don't let the little success you've enjoyed thanks to your older brother's benevolence go to—"

"Basta!" With one arm casually extended, Leonardo stopped Massimo from launching at their father, while with his softly delivered command, he shut his father up. Thankfully, most of the guests had already ventured into the next room when dinner had been announced.

"It is not your company anymore, Silvio. Do not forget that you come out of the clinic for one week per year at my discretion. *Mine*." Leonardo's warning packed no punches. "One word from Massimo and you'll not even see that little freedom."

Silvio left without another word, a little sliver of fear in his puffed-up eyes.

Natalie wondered at how the older man cowered in front of his eldest. Leonardo reminded her of a predator—one who would cock his head and look at you in one breath and then pounce in the next.

But it was the fury on Massimo's face as he turned toward Leonardo that had her chest tight with pressure.

"You told him about a small breach after everything I've done for that blasted company and this family?" he said, his jaw so tight that it seemed to be cast in stone. Pain and anger swirled like shadows in his eyes. "You enabled him for years, you let him abuse…" Massimo turned away, his lean frame vibrating with contained tension.

A whiteness emerged around Leonardo's mouth. Neither had Nat missed his flinch when Massimo had turned on him. "I had to tell him, Massimo. He's the biggest shareholder after you and me. I need…*we* need his help to manage the old cronies on the board if I have to tell them about the breach. You're supposed to be fixing it. Instead…" Leonardo's gaze swung to Natalie.

There was no overt hostility in his dark eyes but she felt like scum on the underside of a rock.

A challenge dawned in Massimo's eyes as he pushed himself into Leonardo's personal space, shuffling Natalie behind his broad shoulders. She fought against the warmth that curled in her chest. If she wasn't careful, Massimo was going to tie her up in knots, swinging from one emotion to the other.

"Would you like to finish that sentence, Leonardo?"

Her heart pumped so hard that Natalie felt it like an ache in her chest.

"Do you know what you're doing, Massimo?"

Massimo didn't back down. "Do you not trust me now?"

The space of a heartbeat, filled with so much tension, before Leonardo said, "Of course I do. I have never trusted anyone more than I do you."

Massimo walked away. Without another word.

If Massimo could be influenced by Leonardo, if things didn't get fixed soon… She shivered at the consequences. Would Massimo ever let it happen?

She turned to Leonardo, her throat strangely achy. "Aren't you going after him?"

Leonardo's head jerked toward her. He'd forgotten about her. And suddenly, she wished she'd just quietly disappeared. "Excuse me?"

She tried to spot Massimo through the crowd. "He's clearly…distressed. Shouldn't you see that he's okay?"

"Massimo is not a child."

"No, but it's clear that he still resents you for what you failed to do when *he was a* child, isn't it?"

The barb pricked the hard face. The all-powerful Leonardo Brunetti flinched again. "Stay out of our family's matters, Ms. Crosetto. If your fate were up to me—"

"But, notwithstanding your father's assumptions,

it's not up to you, Leonardo." He raised a brow at her familiarity with his name. She found she didn't care. "It's up to Massimo.

"Save your threats for someone who hasn't seen the skeletons in your family's prestigious closet."

He studied her with such an intensity that her cheeks burned. "Ah… I see it now."

Nat folded her hands, feeling as small as a bug under a microscope. Her cheap clothes, her untamed hair, even her shoes—nothing was missed by his gaze. "See what?"

"The draw you hold for him. You're obviously talented since you bypassed his design. You're bold, even when cornered, and from that conveniently sad backstory, you're quite the damsel in distress, *si*?

"My brother—" again that flash of concern sat oddly on that ruthless face "—has a weakness for the unfortunate. You're a novelty, Ms. Crosetto. Once that wears off, once he realizes what a liability you are against his ambition, he'll send you where you belong.

"Massimo has an unending thirst, a relentless ambition, to be the master of the world."

"You get your kicks by scaring people who can't defend themselves?"

"I saw that kiss. I saw the way you look at him already, the flash of concern in your eyes when my father spewed his usual poison. This will not end well for you, even if not in jail.

"Tell him the truth and get out of our lives while you still can."

He bowed his head and walked away, leaving Natalie reeling. She'd have ignored his threats if not for the ring of truth in his words. That was two people who were close to him that had warned her about Massimo's ambition.

Suddenly, she felt as lost as she'd felt the morning she'd woken up to discover her father had walked out on her. Wanting to trust and hope that things would right themselves and then being crushed by that hope. Learning to lean on no one but herself. Learning to look out for herself in the big, bad world.

Leonardo Brunetti was right.

Getting out of here without sinking farther into the pit she'd dug herself was the most important thing. She couldn't afford to risk getting closer to Massimo, not even to save herself. She'd no idea how long his leniency toward her would last.

She had to forget that kiss, had to forget Massimo's laughter, the way his eyes glowed when they shared a joke, the sense of challenge he issued to her. She needed to forget the shadows of pain in his eyes when he'd spoken to his father.

She needed to remember that gorgeous, complex man had only looked at her because she had thrown herself into his path by recklessly posing a threat to the most important thing to him—his company.

CHAPTER SIX

IT TOOK A few hours before Massimo emerged from the dark mood a confrontation with his father always left him in. From the quick but ugly jaunt into childhood memories.

He navigated the unlit corridors from his wing to the new guest suites with his rescue dogs, Lila and Hero, limping along by his side, without encountering any more of his family members or their unending drama. On a given day, he could only stomach so much of Greta's relentless carping about the Brunetti dynasty, the increasingly frequent glimpses of loneliness in Alessandra's eyes, Silvio's penchant for spewing poison—a whole year's worth, in a week—and Leonardo's cynicism.

Dios mio, he should be immune to his father's taunts by now.

Instead, he reverted to that emotional, always sick *runt* Silvio used to call him, would still call him if he weren't so terrified of Leonardo.

The boy who'd been heartbroken and unable to protect her when his mother had put up with Silvio's emotional taunts for so long just to be near him, the teenager who'd had to contend with the four walls of his home instead of the outside world and friends, the young adult who'd been terrified that each vicious asthma attack would be the last one.

Only thanks to a miracle drug in his teens had he started getting better, started seeing that he had a future.

The tech world lauded his genius, praised his innovative capabilities that had designed an e-commerce tool worth billions by his nineteenth birthday…and yet, the shadows of that boy still echoed within him.

Computers and the rationality they brought to his tumultuous life, the control and power they'd brought to his hands in a powerless situation, had been his lifeline. An escape from his father's constant verbal abuse away from the eyes of Greta or Leonardo.

That he'd left Natalie to the pack of wolves that was his family had fractured his mood. For all of Silvio's crude remarks, it was Leonardo who was the most dangerous of them.

He grinned, remembering Natalie had no problem standing up to him. No doubt the little minx could hold her own against them. This protectiveness he felt for her…was ridiculous. Unnecessary.

But he couldn't arrest the pulse of excitement as he knocked on the door to her suite. Twice. He was about to knock for the third time when a muffled curse made him grin.

The door opened wide with her leaning against it, eyes mussed with sleep and dark shadows under. Her hair was in such a wild disarray that it was a cloud around her delicate face. The overhead lights she'd switched on outlined her body in caressing lines. A loose T-shirt fell inches above her knees, the neckline baring the delicate crook of her neck.

Innocence and wildness combined together, she made him want to pick her up and crawl into the bed behind her, to drown himself in all that rumpled warmth, to bury his mouth at that pulse at her neck, to discover every rise and dip…

"All the power is in your hands, Massimo."

An uncomfortable sensation skittered in his chest.

She was right. They were not equals.

He wasn't the kind of man who preyed on the weak. He'd never be another Silvio, not even in thought. He couldn't kiss that luscious mouth of hers until he didn't hold her freedom in his hands.

It was imperative that he get to the bottom of the truth. And not just so they could explore this…thing between them. At leisure. No, he needed this threat to dissolve before they could continue talks with Giuseppe Fiore.

But it didn't mean he couldn't enjoy the delectable sight she made. Or rile her up. Or pit his smarts against hers. Or needle her. To give him the truth and more. Natalie was the first woman who challenged him on every level.

He leaned against the archway and smiled at the confusion in her eyes. *"Buongiorno, cara mia."*

"Massimo?" She thrust her fingers through her messy hair, which thrust her breasts up and revealed a little more of her toned thighs. Devoid of makeup or that intractable expression she wore like an armor, he was reminded of how painfully young she really was.

Twenty-two, the report had said. *Cristo*, he'd hate sending her to jail.

"What time is it?"

He grinned. "Four-ten."

"Four-ten when?" she said, grumpy and cute and sexy.

"In the morning."

She looked behind her, peeked into the corridor, then back up at him. Her hand went to the neckline of her T-shirt and tugged it up. Her knees bumped, color climbing up her cheek. "What do you want? I went to bed barely a few hours ago."

"We need to get to work."

"Now?"

"Sì."

"Are you mad? You flew to New York, you barely slept at my apartment, didn't even nod off on the flight and now... Massimo, don't you need sleep?"

He shrugged.

"Well, normal mortals like me do. And that bed is... heaven."

He kept his gaze on hers. "I'll allow you an early night so that you can enjoy the bed some more."

She shook her head. "I'm messed up thanks to jet lag. I barely survived that vicious attack by your family. I don't have enough brain cells to rub together much less—"

"Sì, you will, *cara mia.* Keeping you out of a jail cell depends on your performance in my lab, every day. Your freedom needs to be earned. Starting now. I'll give you thumbprint access to my lab and—"

"Your lab?" Her eyes widened. "You're letting me near a computer?"

"I got your financials back."

She folded her arms and leaned against the door. "And?"

"You have a lot of debt."

White teeth dug into her bottom lip. "Do you believe me now?"

"That you didn't do it for personal gain? *Sì.*" He ran a hand over his neck. "I paid it off."

"What?"

"I paid off your debts."

She moved closer to him, unaware of her movements, the heat from her body licking against his. The skin of her cheeks looked so soft he had to fist his hands. "You paid them off…nine thousand dollars…you paid it off…" She swayed against the door and righted herself. "Why?"

"It was no more than a little change for me. And if it keeps your loyalties directed away from—"

"You think you can buy my loyalty?"

"I'm taking away reasons for you to do something so stupid again. To decouple yourself from a person who led you into jeopardizing your future."

"You didn't pay it off because you felt sorry for me?"

"I'm a businessman first and foremost, Natalie. I'll do anything to protect an asset."

"Not even a little bit relieved that your instincts were right about me?"

He frowned. "I took a calculated risk by bringing you here, whether you took money for the job or not. But trusting some vague instinct, no."

"Does a cold report with numbers make so much of a difference?"

"Of course it does. Numbers don't lie, numbers don't make you lose objectivity. And those numbers will shut up Leonardo's questions about whether I'm sane to be bringing you into the biggest contract we've ever courted.

"Numbers over everything else, *bella mia,* over emotions, over instinct, over weaknesses. Always."

Her face fell. And the question hurtled out of his mouth. "Why does it matter to you that I trust instincts and feelings?"

"What if I can't always provide concrete proof for my innocence?"

Her question came at him like an invisible punch. Reminding him that she stayed a step ahead of him. That for all that innocence in her kiss, she was always thinking of her own survival. That she was just as ruthless about protecting herself and her lies as he was with his company.

"Then I suggest that you don't get involved in anything that might require you to prove your innocence, *cara mia.*" He pushed her into the room, before he was tempted to grill her about the truth, and kiss her when she lied. "Change and meet me outside. I'll show you my bat cave."

She was debt free—like, completely debt free. For the first time in her life.

Unless Massimo was playing games with her...

Wrapping her arms around herself, Natalie stared

at the man walking in front of her, taking in the wet gleam of his jet-black hair, the thick cable sweater lovingly caressing his shoulders and the light blue denim doing wonders to his behind and... God, where was she?

No, Massimo had no reason to trick her. And, she knew, there was no point in arguing with him about paying him back.

Dawn swept into the long corridor through the exquisitely designed arches in ever increasing curtains across the cream marble floor, creeping up and up, slowly illuminating the even more exquisitely detailed murals on the other wall that reached up toward the colorful frescoes upon the domed ceilings.

Every arch and crevice spoke of elegant wealth, of subtle power.

Like he'd said, it was mere change for him.

But for her, suddenly, the world felt like it had opened up into infinite possibilities.

She reached for him as they turned the corner into another hallway. "Thanks, Massimo. I just... You've no idea what it means to me to be debt free."

He tightened his fingers over hers, pulling her to his side. "Tell me."

Surprised, she searched his eyes. "Digging for information?"

"You never stop looking for hidden meanings and agendas, do you?" Exasperation coated his words.

"I'm sorry. It comes with never having had anyone to rely on for so long."

His gaze held hers, understanding and curiosity and so much more in it. "Forgetting your crime and my blackmailing you and all these lies…you're a mystery to me, Natalie. I never could resist one."

She looked away at the beautiful gardens awash in soft pink light. "It means I can start saving instead of just paying interest on my loans. It means I can get out of that dingy studio and maybe find a two-bedroom apartment in a much nicer neighborhood so that Frankie can go to a good public school. It means that I can adopt him much sooner than I had planned. Much, much sooner."

"So you didn't make him up?" he said, a tenderness in his eyes.

She laughed and punched his bicep. "Of course I didn't. When you return my cell to me, I'll show you a pic of him."

"When did you learn about him?"

"About…three years ago." Just the memory of the day put a lump in her throat. "I grew up thinking I was all alone in the world. Apparently, my father, after walking out on me, went and did the same to another woman and her child. This social worker who'd known me when I was in the system…she contacted me when he entered the system.

"I went to see him and Frankie—he was six and so scared. When I held him, I felt as if the universe had done something right in my life for the first time. He… is this adorable, funny, cute little guy. I told him right there that one day he'd come live with me.

"Until then, I'd just drifted from minimum wage job to job. I took out a loan the next day, enrolled in a couple of classes at the community college and…realized it wasn't going to be as easy as I'd thought it would be."

"You had no one to help you?"

She hesitated. The tightening of his jaw told her she'd betrayed herself. The last thing she'd needed after Vincenzo had already loaned her money to get her off the streets when she'd turned eighteen was to beg him for another loan so that she could get a degree.

"No. I didn't. But now...when I get out of this mess, I... So, yeah, thank you." She looked away from him at the wall in front of her.

The wall stretched out far in both directions, reaching up into the domed ceiling. There were murals detailed on the wall, tall, aristocratic figures looking down their long noses—shared by both Massimo and Leonardo—brows drawn together, almost as if sneering at a mere mortal like her walking their hallowed hallways.

Her frown deepened as she spied someone who resembled Leonardo, then Silvio and then Leonardo himself. But no Massimo.

"You're not here," she mumbled, searching for his familiar face among the stern, boorish ones.

"I hadn't earned my place with them when Leonardo invited the artist."

"And now?"

He didn't turn but she saw the tightening of his shoulders just as they reached a building separated from the main villa.

She kept thinking he was part of all this...this dynastic family of his, this alien world that dined on caviar and champagne. But the tension between him and Leonardo, Silvio's thoughtless comments... What if his childhood had been just as awful as hers had been, even in this magnificent home? Even surrounded by family?

The odds he must have had to overcome to build something like BCS when he'd been so sick, when he'd been constantly told he wouldn't amount to much...

She rubbed her face—all traces of sleep gone, confusion roiling through her. Even knowing that Vincenzo hadn't really asked her to steal anything, she didn't want to give up his name. Not after he'd helped her get out of a destructive spiral that would've ruined her life.

Not when he'd never asked for anything in return. Not when he'd been keeping an eye on Frankie's foster situation in the past two years.

Her loyalties, as they were, did belong to Vincenzo.

The very thought while she stood here thanking Massimo for his generosity made her faintly nauseous.

A huge metal door with an electronic thumbprint-access console guarded a huge stone structure that seemed to be built with pure mountain rock. Natalie watched with wide eyes as Massimo pressed her thumb against the console and pushed the door open.

They stood on a ledge with stairs leading down. A thick scent of...grapes lingered in the air as Natalie followed him down. "It smells like...oak and grapes and—"

"It used to be a wine cellar," Massimo said, before he pushed open another glass door. "Leonardo had it designed for my exact specifications. We took out the old stone fireplace, added temperature control and left the original stone structure intact."

Her mouth fell open as Natalie took in the glory of Massimo Brunetti's tech lab. The rock structure provided a magnificent contrast to the high-tech servers stored to the left, while more than three stations on her right housed state-of-the-art supercomputers and glossy monitors she'd only dreamed about. Because of the dark background provided by the rocks, the light from the overhead fixtures gave the whole lab a golden glow.

On the other wall stood a gigantic whiteboard with a leather couch, a snowy white cashmere throw hanging on it and a stand with tech magazines thrown haphazardly. Through the narrow corridor, she saw a small kitchenette with a refrigerator and a small wine rack.

"Wow, this really is your…bat cave. Like the hub of your tech genius."

Teeth digging into his lip, hands tucked into his pockets, he somehow managed to look painfully gorgeous and adorable like a little boy showing off his biggest toys. "You could say that."

"I did wonder at the strangeness of you living at the villa, with your family," she said, laughing. "Doesn't it put a damper on your…extracurricular activities?"

He burst out laughing. "How is that you can strip a layer off even Leonardo but can't speak plainly about sex?"

She hoped the soft light hid her blush. "I'm a complex modern woman."

"That you are.

"I have a flat in Navigli that I use for my…extracurricular activities. Bringing a woman to the villa would only confuse matters."

"Ah…what with the expiry dates and all?"

He shrugged. "I did consider moving out almost a decade ago. When my tech was released and turned into a billion-dollar revenue generator, I had been on a high, raw, so full of myself. I partied so hard," he said with a smile, and she couldn't help but get swept away by his energy. "Very keen to cut my association with my father and Leo and just…the whole lot. But Leo convinced me otherwise. Also, since he was the one who brought in the capital to scale it up in the first place, he had ownership of the IP, too.

"Keeping BCS under the umbrella of Brunetti Finances, Inc. was imperative for Leonardo."

She heard that faint whisper of resentment in his words, the whisper of a boy who'd been measured and found wanting against his older brother. Was he even aware of it?

"Is that when you transformed from gawky geek to sexy stud?" she said, wanting to make him smile.

"Probably, *sì*." Color scored his sharp cheekbones. "I don't think I've ever been complimented in such a… straightforward way." His gaze warmed and he pushed away from the wall. "It provokes me into wanting to return the compliment in the way I know best."

She took a step back, her pulse racing so fast that she felt dizzy. "You could just say I look good, too," she somehow whispered.

"Only you can make an oversize sweater look so sexy. There. But I also believe in giving one thousand percent ROI, *cara mia*."

She looked away from that irresistibly wicked light in

his eyes, the grooves digging in his cheeks. "I'm going to need to carry an oxygen tank with me soon if you continue to look at me like that." She stopped his stride with her palm. A huge mistake. His abdomen was like a slab of rock that surrounded them, and yet somehow warm. "You'll fry my circuits if you kiss me again and I'll be of no use to you."

He laughed and she shivered at the joy and warmth of that sound.

"So this lab…it's a fantasy or what? Those servers, Massimo, I'm salivating at the thought of getting my hands on it."

He switched one on, and yet, his gaze never left hers. "Hard for a man's ego when he has to compete with a machine, *cara mia*. I'd give anything to star in your fantasy. Why is it such a big deal that we both want each other?"

All that rough masculinity leveled at her…her skin prickled with heat. With need.

Still smiling, he leaned against the wall, ankles crossed. Hips slightly thrust up. Denim pulling tight against those rock-hard thighs. His eyes looked blue in this light. Twinkling. Full of naughtiness.

Hair-dusted arms folded at his belly beckoned her. Wet, blue-back hair piled high, gleamed. She had the most overwhelming urge to walk up to him, and kiss that curling mouth. To lean her breasts against those corded arms. To press her hips against his. To tunnel her fingers through his thick hair and pull his head down to her until she could kiss that smiling mouth. To make those laughing eyes turn dark with slumbering desire.

To meet him as his equal, to trust him so fully that she could give herself to him beyond any misgiving or doubt. To live like a normal twenty-two-year-old for once.

She shook her head to rid herself of the stupid longing. They were going to be working here for who knew how long.

"You're a fantasy all right," she said, her words coming out soft and husky. His nostrils flared. "When you look at me like that, when you laugh at things I say, when you touch me, when you…kiss me, it feels as if I was the center of your world. As if you couldn't get enough."

"I can't. Even knowing that you'll run at the first chance, that you'll betray me for some twisted notion of loyalty, that this will only get complicated even more if I do touch you… I still can't stop." He ran a hand over his nape, his voice husky.

Take a step toward me, then, his eyes seemed to say without saying.

She cleared her throat. "But fantasies don't become reality. That's their very nature. Even if you and I had met without my little attack onto your system…we're too different, Massimo. For you that kiss was a pretense. A challenge. A pleasant diversion. A case of kissing the criminal. For me…" She bit her lip, wondering at how easy he made it to be vulnerable with him when all she'd been her whole life was tough.

He had this…insidious way of getting past her defenses.

She couldn't leave her fate to him, yes. But in this,

in this, the only way to protect herself was by showing him her weakness. Trust him to do the right thing. Because all she wanted to do was ask him to make those erotic words into vivid reality. "It was my first kiss."

He came away from the door. "You've never had…" He considered his words, as if this moment was important to him, as if she were important. "You've never been with a man?"

She shook her head, heat crawling up her neck at his prolonged silence.

"Why?"

Again, that feeling of warmth filled her. He never assumed. Massimo always asked.

"It's hard for me trust anyone. Hard for me to let people close. I… I grew up in foster care, got shuffled from home to home. At a young age, I realized that I couldn't count on anyone, that people can bully, berate, be unkind for no reason other than that they have the power to do so." A note of defensiveness crept into her tone, daring him to mock her background, like his family had done.

But all Massimo did was watch her with that intensity. "To give over my security, my feelings, into someone else's power is hard for me. I have friends, of course, but none too close.

"I don't trust easily," she said, wondering if he understood what she wasn't saying.

He did. "And when you give it, it's been earned. Neither will you betray it so easily."

He'd already earned her trust that he'd never harm

her physically, but… She nodded, bracing herself for his anger, for his temper.

"Then it is up to me to make sure you trust me and do what is right for both you and me, *si*? You better believe it, *bella*, I can be very persuasive."

With a wink, he pulled out one of the chairs for her and helped her get settled. Joined her at the next station. Natalie smiled.

"Now, let's forget the outside world, *si*? Show me what you're really made of, Natalie. You have free rein."

She logged into the system, and looked at his network infrastructure. Anticipation built like an inflating balloon in her chest, electrifying her very limbs. "What…what do you want me to do?"

"I want you to mount an attack and show me any more security holes you can find. In BCS and BFI."

"You're not joking."

"No."

"I need a lot of tools and I use open source tech. And get this…some twisted, creative genius named it after a Hindu demon hunter. I need Wi-Fi adaptors that can go into monitor mode and inject packets for penetration testing, a Bluetooth device to monitor traffic, a separate device to install—"

"I have everything you need. If you dare, take me on, Natalie?"

On a wild impulse, Natalie threw her arms around him and took his mouth in a rough kiss. God, he tasted like sunshine and warmth and rationality and wildness, and in two seconds, he turned her awkward fumbling into a knee-bending kiss that stole the very breath from her lungs. His tongue danced sinuously in her mouth, chasing and rolling around hers, his deep groan sending reverberations to the wet place between her thighs.

And it was he that broke it off and settled her back into her seat. "Thank God you did that," he said, rubbing his lower lip with his tongue.

She smiled. "What do you mean?"

"I'm an Italian man in his prime, *bella*," he drawled, thickening his accent. "I cannot have the woman I want panting over some technology more than she does over me. I would have kissed you if you hadn't." He took a deep breath until his chest expanded and his brows were drawn into a leer. "How else would I validate my masculinity?"

Laughter rushed out of her like a firestorm, burning her stomach, bursting through her chest. His gaze filled with laughter, he was the most beautiful man she'd ever seen.

Blushing, Natalie kept her gaze on the screen while the rogue whistled a merry tune as if he'd already won the battle between them.

CHAPTER SEVEN

MASSIMO CAME TO a standstill as he located Natalie in the oval pool, a nightly routine she religiously followed for the last ten days once he called a halt to their workday.

Soft lights illuminated the entire area, including the figure swimming laps in the pool in a blur of yellow. Giant trees artistically grown around the pool gave it privacy and made a paradise that he'd never appreciated fully, before tonight.

Moonlight followed her in splashes of silver on her bare skin, sometimes the dip of shoulder or a toned calf, sometimes that dainty curve of that waist that fascinated him.

All the steam that had built up while Leo had told him of the latest problem he'd come upon with the Brunetti Finances board hissed out of him, all thoughts of business and schemes of revenge and throttling little hackers who lied through their teeth, evaporating like mist.

He'd been so angry with Leo for extending Silvio's stay. But the master strategist that Leo was, he'd expected this situation. Whatever their internal quarrels, it had been essential to present a united front of their family—with Massimo and Leonardo's stalwart presence behind their father's back. The trio of them a force to be reckoned with for any board members with delusions of grandeur.

But that it had come to that…this was on Massimo. This was on his obsession with the little hacker.

Every day he spent with her, he was beginning to lose his mind. Was losing his path a little. And they hadn't even kissed again, not since the last time.

There was such strength, such force, to her personality that he found the fragility of her physical form an endlessly alluring contrast. Ordering Lila and Hero to heel, he settled onto the closest lounger to her, his legs stretched in front of him.

The *swish-swish* of the water and the occasional whisper of a cicada were the only sounds surrounding them. He noticed her focus falter for a few seconds as she noted his presence and his silent scrutiny. Her head went under the water, her arms flailing ungracefully. He pounced to his feet, ready to jump into the pool when she surfaced, spluttering and choking, followed by a litany of inventive curses that chased away the tightness in his throat.

He grabbed a towel and waited while she swam to the edge of the pool. Pushing her hair out of her face, she pulled herself up above the water supported by her forearms over the ledge. Brown eyes shot daggers at him. Kissed by the water, her skin looked so silky smooth that he wanted to run his fingers all over. "You almost made me drown."

"You shouldn't be in the pool if you don't know how to swim, *cara mia*."

"Of course I know how to swim," she said, a note of defensiveness creeping into her tone. "You're watching me without a word and…" He raised a brow and she sighed. "I only learned how to swim recently and haven't perfected my strokes. I was doing perfectly fine until you showed up. You're not good for my focus, Massimo."

That irreverence, that honest but baffled admission… she disarmed him so effortlessly. "You didn't learn as a child?"

"Swimming lessons weren't really a priority for a foster kid." She blew at a wayward curl that was already dry and framed her face. Hair plastered to her scalp, there was a stark simplicity to her face, a soft beauty that was utterly without artifice. "Not when you're shuffled from home to home. I started taking classes at the local Y. When I get out of here, I want to bring Frankie to a beach."

She'd hate it if he felt sorry for her, he knew that instinctively. "The local Y?"

"Y is the YMCA. The lessons are free, for the most part."

A tremble in the slender line of her shoulders made him say, "Get out of the pool."

"Help me up."

He put his hands under her shoulders and pulled her out of the water. The T-shirt and jeans he'd changed into splashed with water but he couldn't give a damn.

Desire fisted low in his belly, rising through him as

quickly as the rivulets of water running down her silky bare skin. The yellow two-piece bikini clung to curves he'd dismissed as meager, only held together by a flimsy string at the nape of her neck. The two triangles of the top held her high breasts like a lover's hands. He could imagine his own hands there, holding them, pushing them up to be savored by his mouth. Could imagine her throwing her neck back, her body arching as he ran his tongue over that rigid nipple pushing against the flimsy fabric. Her thighs were corded with lean muscle, yet somehow so sexy.

Cristo, how could he be so fascinated by her?

He released her hands suddenly. She squealed, her upper body bowing back, her feet slipping on the smooth tiles.

With a curse, he grabbed her. The motion brought her into his body, plastering her to him, from breast to thigh… Time seemed to thunder down to a halt. As if to better equip him to process the amazing sensation of her warm, soft body clinging to his.

"Where did you get the bikini?" he asked hoarsely.

Wide brown eyes gazed at him with liquid longing as he lifted his hands to her shoulders. Rubbed at a drop of water lingering teasingly at the juncture to her neck.

"Alessandra. I didn't pack for a vacation."

"Oversight on my part, *si*. I'll arrange for a wardrobe for you." Polite words to drown the sounds of their harsh breaths.

Her own hands stayed on his chest, his heart thundering like a wild horse under her palm. "No. This pretense that I'm your fiancée…works if they believe I'm different. From my background to my cheap clothes." She swallowed. "That I'm a novelty to you."

Water drops shimmered on her hair like silver lights, spraying him on his face. She was silk under his hands, warmth and feminine hunger.

"And yet… I've never wanted to do all the things I want to do to you, right now. Even knowing that you're probably colluding with an enemy, that you're as complicated as they come." His gaze, with a mind of its own, followed other drops of water running down the valley between those breasts, down the dip and rise of belly and into the bikini bottom. "All I want is to sink to my knees, follow that drop of water across your silky skin. Trail it all the way to the seam of your bikini. To dip my tongue into—"

Her palm on his mouth cut his words off.

He took a long breath, cursing himself for having so little control around her. Tried to push her away from him. But she didn't let go, her arms going tighter around his waist. "Massimo, we agreed we wouldn't do this."

He sighed, the feel of her body molded to his, conversely taking the edge off. Fingers under her chin, he tilted her face up to his. "No, we shouldn't. You're right. Not when you'll hate me when you hear what I have to say."

She stepped back from his hold, fear swirling in the brown depths. "What? What's happened?"

Right and wrong had never been so blurry. Desire and ambition had never been so muddied together. This needed to be resolved before he did anything he would regret later. In his business life and his personal life.

* * *

Natalie shivered even though the glass-enclosed pool was balmy. A luxuriously soft towel instantly covered her shoulders.

He took her willing hands in his. The rough pads of his fingers—another riddle for her to solve—traced the plump veins on the back of her hands. Mesmerizing. Soothing. Arousing. She tugged her hands away. "Massimo, you're scaring me. Just tell me what it is."

"I've given you time. Let you understand that I pose no threat. But I don't have the choice anymore."

"I told you. No one put me—"

"Stop, Natalie!" He stared at her for so long with such intensity that Natalie felt stripped to the bone. After what felt like eternity, he sighed. Resolve tightened the soft curve of his lips. He let go of her hands and she felt the loss so acutely that she had to hide them behind her.

"Would your answer change if I told you the security breach is not an isolated incident?"

Shock made her reaction come in slow, horrifying sweeps. Her stomach plummeted. "What? There were other attacks into BCS's security design?"

"No, that was all you. Only you," he said with a grim smile. Even then, easily acknowledging her brilliance when more than one man scoffed at it. Interestingly, Vincenzo and he had that much in common—an easy acceptance of her talents. "But there have been other things happening at both BCS and its parent company, our finance giant Brunetti Finances, Inc."

She could almost hear the rapid tattoo of her heart. "Like what?"

"Three deals that we had in our pocket fell through. Silvio's colorful, abusive past keeps being recycled by the media and the press. Dragging all of us into the news cycles. Alessandra's personal life, her past, her family in the US, keep getting news time, which, in turn, makes Greta crabbier than usual."

"Your grandmother and Alessandra are close?" she asked, surprised that the crotchety old woman liked and approved of anyone.

"She's not a complete dragon. Nonni was devoted to her second husband. Alessandra's father. Carlo was a good man—he tried to be a good role model to me and Leonardo."

"Didn't quite take?" she said, being drawn into his life. Despite the feeling of a sword hanging over her head. How much had Vincenzo orchestrated? What did he want of the Brunetti family?

Instead of being offended, Massimo regarded it seriously. "He made a world of difference to me. Made Greta and Leo realize what a toxic man my father is. I think…all our lives changed for the better thanks to Carlo. Alessandra shuttled back and forth between her mother in the US and here, and Greta made a lot of effort to make her feel welcome when she finally moved here. For a long time, she even hoped, I think, that either Leo or I would…"

Natalie's heart kicked against her rib cage. "Would what?"

He shrugged. "Would maybe welcome her into the family officially."

"And?" Natalie said, aware of the demand in her tone and unable to quell it. She could even see it from Greta's view. Alessandra would be the perfect bride for one of her grandsons—sophisticated and beautiful and intelligent.

Massimo smiled, his teeth gleaming in the near darkness. Whether at her or the idea of Alessandra with him, she had no clue. "Leo and I like Alex too much to saddle her with us romantically, I think."

Because Alessandra was too good to be played with. Because Alessandra was the kind of woman he respected. The kind of woman to not trifle with.

Whereas Natalie was perfect for an affair.

She felt as if he'd kicked her in the chest. That he was unaware of how awful he sounded didn't help.

Damn it, why did she keep hoping that he'd see her as something more than novelty? Men like Vincenzo and Massimo only had certain uses for women like her, was that it? Another commonality he shared with the man he was hunting.

"So, yes," he went on, unaware of her confusion. "Alex getting dragged into this mess riled Greta, interestingly, even more than the Brunetti name being muddied.

"Anyway, resources for planned projects have been falling through at the last minute.

"And the day before yesterday, there's been a new development. It's why Leonardo kept Silvio here for this long when he knows I loathe it. He had a feeling this was coming."

Natalie had come to hate Silvio's presence, too. The very look in his eyes made her remember all the stuff she was hiding from Massimo. "What new development?"

More than fear gnawing at her insides, Nat hated the doubt in his eyes.

"Massimo, you have to tell me."

"Should I, *cara mia*?"

"You can't think I've got anything to do with it. You've got me locked up here, cut off from the rest of the world."

"Someone leaked about the breach to one of the board members. Forcing our hand to come clean to the entire board. You can imagine how that went down. That our clients' information wasn't stolen becomes irrelevant, do you see?"

"It can't be anyone else?"

"The board member who accused Leonardo of hiding this from them, this is not the first time he's tried to cause trouble for Leo, not the first time he's strategized to oust him from the board. He's not going to give up his source, either. But don't you think it's a little too convenient that of all the board members, Mario Fenelli was the one who's been told about the breach? The only people who knew were me, Leo, Silvio, you and the person who leaked it."

Dread so complete enveloped Nat's limbs that she felt frozen. "Wait, you think someone is sitting there strategizing all this?"

"Yes."

Jesus, what was Vincenzo doing? It wasn't bad enough that he'd dragged her into the middle of this, now he'd gone ahead and leaked the news about the... breach?

Massimo's gray gaze stayed far too calm. Far too intense on hers. "It's too much of a coincidence to think otherwise. So far, nothing has been so bad as to bring us down. Not too much of a financial hit for BCS or Brunetti Finances. Until now, with the breach so cleverly exposed where it could do maximum damage to Leo. It feels almost as if—" he frowned, clearly struggling with something "—someone is trying to figure out—" his intense gray gaze pinned her, leaving her no way to escape "—what would hurt us the most."

The truth of his statement hit her like a lash. He ran a thumb up and down her cheek. She sank into the featherlight touch, desperate for the warmth of it, despite the tension surrounding them. Despite the lines she'd drawn between them. "Maybe you didn't know what you were getting into. I will allow for that. Maybe you were never meant to know more about this. But now it's up to you to make the right choice."

He was not quite the stranger from the first night again—cold, powerful and a little bit frightening. But neither was he the man who had laughed with her, the man who had kissed her as if she were the only anchor in his storm.

Was Vincenzo behind the other attacks, too? Why? Why was he targeting Massimo and Leo? How could he involve Nat in something so underhanded knowing how precious Frankie was to her? How could she give him up to Massimo when she owed him so much over the years?

"You have a week, Natalie. I need a name. I need this to end."

"Or else what, Massimo?" she demanded, a shiver in her very words.

"Or else I will let Leo handle the situation. I would let him do the dirty work of sending you to prison, let him be the villain. See, I'm no one's hero, *bella mia*. In fact, I'm even worse than Leo. Because Leo accepts the reality of what he is.

"I...on the other hand, like to pretend, as long as it's convenient and easy to do, that I'm better than him. That I'm better than my father."

CHAPTER EIGHT

HEART THUMPING AGAINST her chest like a bird trapped in a cage, Natalie pressed her thumb against the electronic access panel. The soft *ping-ping* of the panel as it turned green had the same effect on her as a meteor hitting the earth might have. Her belly swooped and her sweaty palms slipped as she pulled the door to the lab open.

Just thinking about the gray gaze looking at her as if she were an unknown criminal, someone not deserving of even the little consideration he'd shown her, she shivered, even in the thick woolen sweater she had borrowed from him on that first day. Walking to the terminal he'd set up for her, she pulled the loose neckline by stretching it and buried her nose in the soft wool.

The scent of Massimo seeped into her breath, into her blood, calming the panic in her muscles. An almost hysterical laugh bounded out of her mouth, echoing in the huge space. How strange that here she was planning to betray his trust again and it was the scent of him that calmed her.

She watched her reflection in the huge monitor as the system booted. Two days and countless conversations in her head hadn't made this decision easier or given her a different solution.

Yes, Vincenzo was a sneak and a master strategist and he was completely in the wrong for doing what he was against the Brunettis and for putting her in the middle of it. And no, she still couldn't betray him. Which meant she had to look out for herself.

Thoughts jumbled, tangled, piled and raced through her head while her fingers raced over the keyboard, creating the bot program that would search all of Massimo's cyber infrastructure for the proof against her. For the record he'd diligently put together to track her and nail her.

When her program found it, it would destroy the proof that he could use to send her to jail. Come tomorrow morning, Massimo would have nothing on her.

Except pure hatred.

Sweat gathered on the nape of her neck, the lab suddenly feeling like a jail itself, taunting her for what she intended to do.

God, she couldn't bear to see the disgust and the shock of betrayal in his eyes, couldn't bear for him to see the reality of what she was.

If she did this, there was no going back. He wouldn't trust her ever again; he wouldn't smile at her, wouldn't laugh with her, wouldn't kiss her ever again.

She buried her face in her hands and groaned.

And yet, to leave her security to the whims of a man, even if the man had shown her kindness and generosity, a man who prized his ambition over everything else…

it went against every grain of instinct that had helped her survive for so long.

God, she was tired of fighting, so tired of being tough.

All she wanted, desperately needed, was to leave this lab, this place, this man who threatened her security on so many levels.

She had to.

The soft chirrup from his wristwatch grabbed Massimo's attention as he waited in the foyer for everyone to arrive.

An alert from the access log for his lab.

He frowned, but pushed the notification away with a swipe of his finger. Right now, he had more important things on his mind. Already, he was far too distracted and excited about the prospect of seeing Natalie. Eerily, it was the sensation he remembered from being a skinny geek, hoping the girl he liked would notice him at university.

Wait till you see her tonight.

The pithy text from Alex almost two hours ago while he'd been finishing his workout had filled him with all kinds of anticipation. He had trouble enough to focus when Natalie was close even when she wore her usual skinny jeans and any old T-shirt. Even now, he could recall the sight of her pulling on his thick sweater, flashing him her belly, by simply closing his eyes. Oversized, hanging off-shoulder, it should have looked anything but sexy on her. And yet, when he'd spied her burying her nose in the fabric, a smile playing around her lips, he had gone hard as stone.

Cristo, she revved him up so quick just by being present. Who knew what she would do to him if she actually dressed up for him.

Tonight was the night of the annual charity gala that the Brunettis hosted at the Galleria Vittorio Emanuele II. The one evening that Leo and Greta insisted they present a united front to Milan and the world at large. Much as Massimo preferred to toil in his lab over playing political games with the most powerful families of Milan, tonight was one night even he didn't dare buck tradition.

Giuseppe Fiore would be there, and Massimo wanted to see him in a setting away from the usual meetings. Without being surrounded by all his yes-men with their own agendas to push.

The man was an incisively clever businessman, noncommittal to the last moment, and Massimo needed to see if the news of the security breach had reached Giuseppe's ears. If it had, he would have to do damage control. Both on the business front and the personal. And having Natalie on his arm, he hoped, would smooth over any drama with Gisela.

No one who could see them together could doubt he had only eyes for her. The decision of what to do with her—on so many levels—had begun to give him sleepless nights.

"Keeping an eye on her is one thing, Massimo," Leo said. "Scratching an itch is one more indulgence. But letting her access your security designs for the Fiore contract…isn't that a bit much?"

Massimo had expected this confrontation the same evening that he'd introduced Natalie to his family. That Leo had waited a whole two weeks when his ruthless brother never hesitated to cut anyone, whether personal or business.

He frowned. Was Natalie right?

Had Leo kept away because of Massimo's harsh words? Was it possible that his accusations had hurt his brother?

"Stay out of this, Leo."

"I stayed out of your lab, literally, for ten days, Massimo. Left you to indulge in whatever you…want with her. Hasn't that been enough?"

"Do not speak of her that way," Massimo gritted through his teeth, the very idea of Natalie as some kind of toy to be used disturbing him on multiple levels. Even though that's what he'd always used women for. Meaningless, casual affairs so that nothing could distract him, nothing could become an obstacle to his ambition. "She's been working around the clock with me to fortify the security of BCS. She's brilliant. If I can get her to commit to us, she'll be an asset to us on the Fiore banking project."

"Despite the fact that what she did might jeopardize our chance to get the contract? Before we clear up the problem she created, Massimo?" Leo set his perceptive gaze on Massimo. "She committed a crime. She refuses to tell you why or the name of the man responsible. You conveniently set all that aside because you want her.

"It's a little too close to Silvio's behavior—"

"Natalie isn't like any other woman you or I know."

Leo's eyes widened. "You like her."

The words washed over Massimo.

He did like her. For the first time in his life, it went beyond physical attraction. He'd threatened her that he would turn her over into Leo's hands, but could he, really?

Protecting a woman who was determined to keep her secrets over sound business decisions... For the first time in his life, Massimo wondered at the weakness that Silvio had always said resided in him. Was this it? Was this...unwillingness to threaten everything she held precious a weakness in him?

No! It couldn't be.

Leo pushed his fingers through his hair as if he'd discovered a bigger problem to solve. "I never thought you would be a fool for a woman."

"I'm not marrying her, Leonardo. I just refuse to take advantage of her."

"You really can't believe that act of innocence."

No, he didn't think Natalie was unaware of her own culpability. Or that she would ever stop looking after her own interests first.

But her shock when he'd told her about the other attacks had been genuine.

They'd spent days fortifying BCS's security design, patching up flaws that Natalie found with an incisively brilliant mind. He'd seen her brilliance with security design, her sheer joy in playing with it. He'd also seen her struggle with what he'd told her. She'd asked him questions again and again, sifting through detail, trying to connect the dots. He could almost see the picture emerge in her head last evening. See the conflict in her brown eyes, eyes that had never been able to hide anything.

Leo turned his gaze to Massimo. There was still that wariness in his eyes. As if Massimo were a stranger. As if Massimo could attack again and possibly hurt him.

His brother—the powerful, cynical, ruthless Leonardo Brunetti—hurt by Massimo's words? If not for Natalie, he'd have never seen it.

"If she's poor, buy the truth from her," Leo said into the awkward silence. "We need to know who's behind all this. She's our only lead. Nothing else is panning out."

"Natalie is not the type to be bought." She was brilliant, and funny and naive and more than a little defensive about her background and a whole lot loyal. Discovering the complex depths to her only made her even more interesting to him. Made him to want to protect her. Made him wonder what a man had to do to earn that loyalty.

"How do you not see that's worse? It means her loyalty has already been given to another man."

"She'll tell me the truth."

"Why?"

"I don't know, okay? I'm putting all the pressure I can on her," Massimo said, hating that he had no better answer or way of getting it. Hating that he was acting weak. Was he being foolish enough to hope that she'd open up to him eventually? When did being fair turn into weakness? Why the hell didn't the woman just save her skin? "Leave it, Leonardo, *per favore.*"

The words he really wanted to say to Leo lingered on his lips. He cleared his throat. "Have you considered it might be someone Silvio cheated or abused or plain pissed off? Both you and I know his sins are numerous. Against many."

"That's the first thing I thought of." His brother rubbed his face. "I'm looking into it."

"*Bene.* I thought you might have forgotten what kind of a man our father is."

"I tolerate him better than you do, *sì.* Does not mean I forget what he is capable of."

Massimo nodded. *Cristo*, emotions were hard to put into words. But he had never shied away from the truth, either. "I owe you an apology."

Leo jerked his head up.

"For blaming you for Silvio's actions. All these years."

Whiteness emerged around Leo's mouth. As if his biggest fear about their relationship had come true. "Massimo, you didn't... I have never held that against you."

"*No?*" He smiled at his brother's uncharacteristic lenience. "Then you should. You were just as much a child as I was. Just as much brainwashed as I was. When I see him, I only see the bully. The insecure, pathetic narcissist who made Mama's life hell.

"The face he showed you...it's much more dangerous— it's charming and loving and you had to see beyond and beneath all that. Until Natalie pointed it out to me, I... I didn't realize how much that resentment still festered. How easily I could believe that you would choose him over me."

Leo's eyes held a wealth of regret before he looked away. "I… I wish I had realized sooner. Massimo. I wish…"

Massimo rubbed his brother's shoulder. "It's in the past. And even knowing it, Mama had never been able to stop it. But that's the kind of woman Natalie is, do you see?

"I'm not saying she's not culpable. Even as you advise me to incarcerate her, knowing your opinion, she made me see how much resentment I still harbored toward you. How much I pitted myself against you. How much it hurt you. Even knowing the both of us for so many years, can you see Greta doing anything like that? Calling me on it.

"As if I had to prove I was better than you. As if I were still in competition with you for his affections," he finished, disgusted with himself.

"You're a much better man than me, Massimo."

"I think I forgot that."

Leonardo raised a brow in mock arrogance, his mouth split into a smile. "Good to see you back on form."

Massimo laughed at this dry wit. How had he not seen that his brother showed this side of himself only to Massimo?

"No, that's not right. It's not a competition between you and me," Massimo corrected himself. "I'm my own man. There are, of course, shadows of Silvio in me, but Mama and Carlo tried their best to cancel that out, I think." He looked at Leonardo and realized how lucky he had been, in a way, that Silvio had shown his true colors from the beginning.

"Now I can sleep better, knowing that whoever is causing this at least won't come between you and me." Leo gestured between them.

Massimo nodded, ashamed that he had caused Leonardo that fear. "We'll find a way, Leo. Even if—"

His brother's gaze turned away from Massimo, a pithy curse flowing from his mouth. Massimo frowned and turned.

His own intake of breath sounded like a shout in the quiet lounge.

Dressed in a gold evening dress that left her slender shoulders bare, Natalie walked down the steps. The bodice of the dress was two wide strips of silky gold fabric that roped up from her midriff, crisscrossing, to cover her breasts, like a lover's demanding hands, before the ends tied behind her graceful neck. Under the bright lights of the crystal chandelier overhead, the valley between her breasts shimmered, drawing his gaze.

Desire made his muscles tight. He had the most overwhelming urge to run the tip of his tongue there, before uncovering the plumpness of her flesh. The dress, designed to make men salivate, left the sides of her midriff bare, showcasing more bare silky skin, the sexy dip of her waist flaring into her hip.

Her glorious hair was tied into a knot at the back of her head, unruly, wavy tendrils falling forward to frame her jawline. Her eyes shimmered with a false brightness while her mouth, painted a wild red, curved into a tremulous smile. The pulse at her neck fluttered rapidly.

The slinky fabric fell to her ankles, shimmering with every step, the thigh-high slit in it revealing glimpses of a toned thigh. Three-inch heels finished her outfit. One hand anchored on the banister while she pressed the other palm into her belly.

She'd never be sensationally beautiful like Gisela or Alessandra. But her beauty was more than skin-deep. It lured with those intelligent eyes, made him laugh with that beguiling mouth, stripped him to the core by peeling off her own layers. But in that dress that highlighted the innate sensuality of her slim figure, delicate cheekbones carefully highlighted by clever makeup, she looked incredibly fragile, wild. As if one touch from him would mar her innocence.

She came to a halt at the last step, her gaze holding his, inviting and teasing and alluring. Lust spread through his limbs like drugged honey.

She had chosen the dress with him in mind. Her expressive eyes said as much without coyness, without artifice. She let him see the desire in her eyes, demanded he do the same. Never had a woman continually stunned and stripped Massimo to his core like Natalie did.

"Do you still believe her innocent?" Leo's voice at his back sounded eerily like his own beneath the desire drumming through his veins. "She stands there like a Christmas present waiting to be unwrapped by you. She's incredibly bold, such a tempting challenge, *sì*. What man can resist such open invitation? If this is not an attempt to seduce you into granting her freedom just when you tell me you're tightening the screws on her…then I will never speak against her again."

Massimo tightened his jaw, fighting the atavistic urge to punch his older brother, to hide Natalie away from his gaze.

She was dressed to draw a man's gaze and keep it.

Why was she into him now when nothing had changed, if not to seduce him into granting her freedom? Was he a fool to have trusted her this far?

CHAPTER NINE

Natalie stared around her openmouthed, even after two hours, at the opulent grandeur that was Galleria Vittorio Emanuele II. The two iron-and-glass-covered walkways met at a central piazza below the grand, wide glass dome. The mosaic on the floor, depicting so many patriotic symbols of Italy, glittered under the bright lights.

Large circular tables covered with snowy white linen and adorned with beautiful floral arrangements that combined white orchids with bamboo were placed along the four branches of the gallery, welcoming eight guests on each. Each table, she'd been informed by Greta, cost five thousand euros, which would then be donated to a charity project offering meals to people in need throughout Milan.

There were designers from world-famous fashions labels, tech business leaders and even the mayor of Milan in attendance.

Massimo's subdued mood, something she couldn't get a handle on since she'd arrived at the lounge where he'd been waiting with his family, couldn't take away her attention for too long. The glorious setting and the dazzling gala felt like a stay on an execution that would come tonight.

But even the fear of where this night would end couldn't rob her appreciation of the setting. It was as if she had entered a different era—a different world. As the formal seated dinner finished, Massimo silently studying her responses all through it, the guests started wandering. Scents of the bitter coffee and decadent chocolate lingered in the air. A pianist sat in a corner, his fingers flying over the ivory keys, Beethoven's Sonata filling the air.

The Galleria, she'd been educated by a smiling Gisela in halting English, was the very heart of the city that married an intricate and complex historical period of Milan with technical, engineering and industrial accelerations. She wished she had her cell phone so that she could capture the glittering night and share it with Frankie later. To look secretly at night when she wished she was part of this world again.

Only families like the Brunettis—power and connections built into their very blood—could indulge the idea of using the Galleria, a cornerstone of Milan's history, for a private charity dinner.

During the day it was the site of the much-lauded Milanese luxury shopping, with many prestigious labels and brand shops. Even without any money to spare, Natalie wished she'd seen the place during the day. Wished she'd begged Massimo to bring her out for a trip to see the city.

They both needed a break, anyway—from being

cooped up in the lab for seventeen-hour days and from the tension that seemed to corkscrew around them every time they looked at each other. Damn Vincenzo, the man was like an apparition between them, choking the air around them.

Natalie stole the chance to wander away from the Brunettis. She could already more than tolerate or ignore Greta's snide commentary, which almost seemed to be by rote. She laughed, surprised at the thought that Alessandra might have had a word with the old woman before she had left this morning after she'd seen Natalie crawl out of the lab like a thief, tense and shaking. Tongue-in-cheek, Natalie had attributed it toward nervousness for this party.

She was about to make her escape when Massimo clasped her arm, and coiled it through his own. The tight cast of his jaw silenced her protest. "I want you to meet Giuseppe Fiore and his CTO."

She nodded, her heart beating rapidly at the frost in his eyes. Had he already discovered what she'd done this morning? How? She hadn't triggered the program to start until this evening. Even before she'd tweaked it again.

She let out a soft gasp when his thigh pressed against hers, the heat from his body a warm caress. His chest pressed into the side of hers, grazing her breast, setting nerve endings on fire. His fingers landed on her bare skin at her waist to steady her, searing her skin. Neither did he stop. He spread his palm out, maximizing the contact, his fingertips digging into her skin, the gesture utterly possessive. Breath coming out shallow, she raised her eyes to his. "Massimo?"

"You're playing with fire, *bella*. Are you prepared to burn?"

She could do nothing but stare into the desire he didn't hide.

Even seeing the beautiful Gisela on her father's arm, in a striking emerald creation, completely in her element as they joined them, commenting about casual acquaintances that Natalie would never know, sharing inside jokes, falling into rapid Italian that Nat had no way in hell of following—even that went over her head in contrast to the all-consuming possessiveness of Massimo's hold.

After all, her job tonight had been to hang on to Massimo with a doe-eyed adoring look that telegraphed to everyone that he was taken. For his part, Massimo was perfect in playing the adoring fiancé role.

Neither did she miss the way Gisela sidled to his side every chance she got, the way she put her hand over Massimo's chest, the way she leaned into him. While he didn't encourage Gisela, neither did Massimo look troubled by the way Gisela touched him without his consent. As if he were Gisela's property just because he was doing business with her father.

Natalie stayed by his side as more guests joined them and with effortless charm he soothed ruffled feathers about the continuing threats to Brunetti Finances. For a technical genius, he didn't talk down to any of them or dismiss the questions that Giuseppe's CTO raised as inconsequential. She couldn't help but admire the clear, concise way he explained the security breach— her hacking attack.

Natalie stiffened when he introduced her to them, expounding on her brilliance with cyber security design to the older man, surprising both him and Natalie.

When Giuseppe had asked for Natalie's experience and qualifications, Massimo smoothly slipped it in that it was Natalie that had launched the attack on BCS but very cleverly left it in the air for Giuseppe to think that she had done so at Massimo's behest and somehow the news had leaked of his own measures to tighten the security.

It was a brilliant business move—using mostly the truth, he calmed Giuseppe's fears about the security attack and yet proved that he had everything under control with Natalie at his side. Massimo might detest the business side of things, but it didn't mean he was any less of an astute businessman than Leonardo. She saw the flash of shock and admiration in Leo's eyes as Giuseppe bought it all.

The older businessman was much more gracious than his daughter for he wished Natalie well, congratulating her on landing "a most brilliant young man."

Once Giuseppe seemed to be satisfied, Natalie pushed away from Massimo and he let her go. She drifted from group to group, slowly making her way toward the bank of elevators a uniformed waiter directed her to.

She had held up her end of the pretense for tonight. Now, she waited for the ax to drop.

Voices thinned and drifted into soft whispers as Natalie made her way toward a smaller corridor that held the elevators to the HighLine. She'd heard walking on the HighLine over the Galleria would be like touching the sky. And right now, she couldn't bear to be around a man whose opinion was coming to matter too much to her.

The elevator car opened and Natalie stepped in. Before the doors closed, a handmade Italian leather shoe stopped them. His broad shoulders pushing the doors open, Massimo stepped into the car. Natalie pressed her hands against the cool metal, to puncture the tension filling the enclosed space instantaneously. Her belly swooped, more to do with him than the car rushing up.

"Running away, *cara mia*?"

"I just wanted to look around," she whispered. And then hating the quaver in her voice, she straightened her shoulders. "To get away from the woman fawning over you. That's allowed, isn't it?"

When he punched the button to stop it, she swallowed. "Then it's also allowed that I follow my errant fiancée, *si*? At least to make sure she's not meeting another man in secret?"

Natalie paled. "You can't seriously think I've arranged to meet someone when you've cut me off from everyone. You…don't think like that. Did Leonardo plant that in your head?"

His jaw tightened. "Leave my brother out of this."

"Massimo, why are you so angry? You've been in a foul mood all night."

"Why did you dress up tonight—" his gaze roamed over her chest, and then pulled up, a banked fire in it "—when it took me three days to convince you that I need you here at the gala at all?"

That's what this was about?

"I didn't want to embarrass you or you to be ashamed of me. Even if it's all a sham, I didn't want you to realize I was beneath all those women. I wanted…"

To appear to be worthy of you. The words stuck in her throat.

How had he become so important to her that looking out for herself felt like a betrayal to him?

"You wanted what?"

God, she was sick and tired of being twisted by her own feelings.

She clasped his jaw, tugging his head down to meet her eyes. Never in her life had she felt so vulnerable, so willingly weak. Only this man did that to her. He made her wish for things that would always be out of her reach. He made her wish she was…different. And that was the worst sort of thing to do to herself. "I wanted to look like I belonged on your arm."

The rough stubble in his skin sent longing unfurling through her stomach. She dipped her face, burying it in the crook of his neck. The scent of his skin seeped into her very breath. Her hands crawled up from his waist, to his chest, touching him, exploring him.

His heart thudded under her palms, his harsh breaths feathering through her hair. Need and fear drove her to do things she wouldn't have dreamed of. Instinct spurred her on. Pressing her chest to his, she vined her arms around his lean waist. Inched her legs to be cradled between his.

Gray eyes darkened into the color of the sky during a storm. His breath came slow and shallow. Burrowing herself into him, she felt the stirrings of his erection against her belly. Hardness and heat.

She met his gaze, then stroked the tip of her tongue at the seam of his lips. "Kiss me. Please, Massimo."

"Why?"

She laughed. The soft sound filled the small space. "After all the teasing and taunting of the last two weeks, now, when I ask you…"

A vein in his temple throbbed. "Why the sudden change in mind, then?"

"Because when you kiss me, I forget everything else. I forget the whole damned world and what is right and what is wrong. When you kiss me, I'm not so tightly wound anymore. I'm not scared." She sent her hands seeking into his hair, and tugged his head down. Pressing her mouth to the sides of his, she drowned herself in him. With the tip of her tongue, she licked at the soft lower lip, stroked it along the carved line, from this end to the other until the taste of him was embedded in her blood. "Don't ask questions, Massimo. Please. Just for now. Just for a few moments.

"Imagine that the outside world—your company, your family, your ambition—none of those exist. Imagine you met me that first night in the cyber club and we connected. Imagine that I came to you willingly, desperate for the pleasure you could give.

"What would you do with me if I were all yours?"

What would you do with me if I were all yours?
Natalie's question unlocked all the desires Massimo had been struggling to bury since he'd set eyes on her.

The press of her mouth against his, hungry and soft, seeking and searching, innocent and mind-numbingly addictive, destroyed the anger that had been brewing at her conniving intentions tonight. Right and wrong had never been so blurry.

Cristo, he was such a cliché of a man.

The slide of her body against his, his chest crushing her breasts, her long legs tangling with his, the way her soft belly grazed his thickening erection—it was heaven and hell. His hands crawled into her hair, tugging and pulling.

Yes, she thought to seduce him with a motive, with a goal.

Who said she would attain her goal?

Who said she would win in this game she'd started between them?

Who said he was going to grant her her freedom?

And not just because keeping Natalie around was good for BCS, even for the hundred-billion Fiore contract. Not because she still was the only lead they had in discovering the mastermind that was strategizing all this.

He wasn't going to let Natalie go, not for a long while yet. Because he wanted her brilliant mind around. Because he wanted to explore this thing between them, see this through to the end.

Acknowledging that freed him from his own guilt. From his own restrictions.

He pressed his mouth to her shoulder, dragged it to the tender nook of her neck, licked the pulse hammering away madly. Desire was a deafening drumbeat pulsing through his body. He opened his mouth, planting a wet kiss before sinking his teeth into the supple flesh, tugging it and releasing it until she was squirming against him. Burrowing into him as if she meant to reside under his skin. She tasted sweet and salty and soft and silky. Curling his fingers at her neck, he jerked her head back, until her spine curved, until he was all she could see.

Brown eyes muddied with desire stared up at him. Her glorious hair was coming away, rumpling all that innocence. Her chest rose and fell shakily, her nipples tight points poking against the slinky fabric. "Are you sure you want this, *bella mia*?" he said, desire deepening his tone, struggling to hold on to the last thread of sanity.

"Of all the rights and wrongs between us, this is the only thing I'm sure of, Massimo."

Pulling her up, Massimo took her mouth like a drowning man. Dove into the soft cavern of her mouth like a starving man. With rough movements, he turned them around, until her back was against the wall and her front was plastered to him.

She came into the kiss with a groan that pulled at his control, that reverberated inside him like a bloody gong going off. As if schemes and seductions were nothing compared to her hunger for him. Her voracious mouth. Her kisses tasted like honesty and passion and innocence and everything that aroused him, that tied him up in knots, about his little hacker.

"Anything, Massimo. Tonight, anything for you," she whispered in a litany, sinking into his kiss, sinking those misaligned teeth into his lower lip. Hard. Pain flashed at the edges of his consciousness, crystallizing the pleasure she drew from him even more. A feral groan ripped from his mouth as she swiped that tart tongue over the hurt she gave him.

He licked and nipped at her bottom lip, before thrusting his tongue inside. She was sweet, and hot, and *Cristo*, she was a quick learner the way she pressed her tongue against his when he went seeking. His hands continued their own foray, cupping her buttocks, squeezing her hips, learning every dip and swell, tracing the contours of her back before returning to her bottom again.

With his mouth, he trailed the silky softness of her cheek, her neck, licked at the pulse again before sucking it into his mouth. He was being rough, rougher than he'd ever been with a woman on their first time, rougher with a woman who'd so bravely admitted that his kiss had been her first.

Her little pants and mewls were like beacons guiding him, giving him a map to her body, a key to driving her as mindless as him. When he snuck his hand under the slit and cupped her bare buttock, she moaned.

When he buried his mouth in her neck and sucked at her skin, she pushed herself into his touch.

When he shifted the flimsy fabric of her dress away to reveal the globe of her breast that had been playing peekaboo with him all evening, she shuddered in his hold.

When he rubbed the pad of his thumb over the plump pink tip he discovered, she sank her fingers into his hair and tugged.

When he licked the knotted tip begging for his caress, she ground her belly against his erection. When he swirled his tongue over and over around the pink peak, she let loose a string of curses that were music to his ears.

When he took her nipple into his mouth and caressed it with press of his tongue, when he closed his mouth around the peak and pulled, she came away from the wall, a litany of cries falling from her lips.

For every small action of his, she reacted like the sky lighting up, like thunder that shook the ground. With explosive passion. With unbound enthusiasm. When he moved his hand from her rounded bottom that filled his hand oh-so-perfectly to the line of her hip and tugged at the string of her thong, she stilled.

"Massimo?" she whispered, a wealth of desire and a flicker of doubt in it.

He covered the mound of her sex with his palm, the raspy brush of hair, the warmth of her stinging him like electric current. *Dios mio*, he didn't remember a time when he'd been more turned on. He lifted his head and kissed her. Softly, this time, slowly, letting their mouths dance to the tune their bodies demanded, willing her to trust him. In and out, he plunged his tongue, in a rhythm his erection desperately needed. "You're so responsive, *cara mia*. I want to kiss, lick and touch you everywhere."

Eyes so wide that he could drown in them filled with sudden shyness. "Here? Shouldn't we go home?"

He smiled, the sight of her swollen lips, lipstick all smudged, the dilated pupils, her hair in a wild disarray, her pulse fluttering—a visual feast he'd never be able to forget.

A sight that made every possessive instinct in him flare into life. The thought of any other man seeing her like this, knowing this intimacy with Natalie, being the recipient of her smiles and her joy and her brilliant mind… *Cristo*, where was this possessive instinct coming from? Why was he muddying sex with emotion?

"Massimo?" she said, prodding him softly. Kissing him, dueling her tongue with his, just as he'd taught her mere minutes ago.

"Here, Natalie," he said, resolve filling his very blood. She would be his, only his. Somehow, he'd make it happen. "I can't f—" He tempered his words, now, today.

Another day, another night, when he showed her how it could be between them, when she reveled in this heat between them, when she realized she couldn't live without him inside her, again and again, when she understood the power she could have over him and he over her, then he wouldn't curb his language. Then he would use the filthiest words he wanted and take her every which way.

But for now, this trust she gave him that was so hard for her to do was a gift. A gift he intended to prize above all else.

"I can't be inside you here. Not without protection." She colored so innocently that he took her bruised mouth again in a rough kiss. "But I'm desperate to see you come, to hear the sounds you make when you do. When we walk out of here, and the boring monotony of that party makes me want to pluck my eyes out, the sounds and scent of your orgasm will be my strength to get to the other side."

She smiled, desire lighting up her eyes into a thousand colorful beams. A little naughty. A lot willing. Her hands trembled as she straightened his jacket. "Beneath all that ambition, you're a wicked man."

She was laughing when he took her mouth again in a kiss—a sound that seemed to burrow into his veins, and it was the most joyous, arousing thing Massimo had ever heard in his life.

Her mouth matched his this time, hungrily licking and nipping, teeth banging, tongues tangling. As if he and his kisses and caresses weren't just to meet the needs of her body but to fill her soul, as well. As if it were a challenge she was laying down at him, to meet her fully.

He ravaged her mouth roughly all the while pulling her up, until his hand lodged under her thigh, tugging her leg up, opening her center up for him, until his cock was pressed into the hot V between her thighs.

Goaded by instinct, he rocked his hips into the welcoming groove. Pleasure burst over his skin like a million little charges had burst into life. Their mingled groans filled the air with an erotic thrum.

Cristo, he wanted to be inside her now. Without protection. Without caution. Need was like a thousand needles under his skin, stealing away rationality, urging him toward making promises to her. Promises that would chain her to him.

Promises that would have given him nightmares a mere month ago.

Promises of a future he'd never once in his life even considered as an option.

Instead, he sent his fingers seeking her wet heat. Anticipation had nothing on reality when he pushed her thong to the side and found her sex. *Cristo*, she was willing and wanton. For him. Only for him.

Moaning, she threw her head back when he found her clit. Jerked as if a lightning storm had hit her when he rubbed her moisture at her entrance, when he slowly penetrated her with one finger.

She was a wet, hot sheath, and every inch of him tightened, imagining how she good she would be around his cock. Sweat beaded on his forehead, restless heat clamping every muscle. "*Merda*, you're tight, so ready, *cara mia*. Look at me, Natalie. Tell me how it feels."

Eyes glazed, she looked down, her two front teeth buried in her lower lip. Her hands descended to his shoulders, her forehead pressed into his shoulder. "It feels…new, strange. Achy, Massimo. Like there's a fever inside me. Please…don't stop."

"That's my brave little hacker," Massimo whispered against her mouth while he pushed another finger into her and stretched her slowly. Every inch of his body corkscrewed with tension, crying for release. He kept his thumb pressed against her clit while working a slow rhythm with his fingers. "Move over my fingers, *cara mia*. Tell me what feels good, learn what sets your body on fire."

She came up and away from him, her body tense and

shaking, soundless cries falling from her lips. He used his other hand to cup her breast, loving the stiff poke of her nipple at his palm. Color filling her cheeks, hands clinging to his shoulders, she caught on to the rhythm of his fingers. He plumped and petted one breast after the other, rubbing and rolling her nipples, watching her—fascinated, hungry, obsessed with how sinuously she moved, how quickly she learned what made it good for her, how greedily she demanded he move the heel of his palm to exert counterpoint pressure to the slick movements of his fingers.

Panting and moaning, writhing against his fingers, release came upon her, sending her slender body into spasms. Her skin shimmered with a damp sheen, her eyes heavy-lidded. She opened her eyes and held his gaze with such crystal clarity, such a possessive light, tossing them both up into the intensity of the moment.

Dios mio, would he ever have enough of this?

He helped her ride out her climax, her pleasure feeding his, until she arrested his wrist, and flopped onto him like a spent storm. Arms cradling her, he held her while she clung, whispering inanities, telling her what a beautifully wild creature she was.

He leaned his forehead into her shoulder, the musky scent of her arousal filling his very breath. This was not him. This man blinded by lust, egged on by the need for possession.

BCS was his life, his goal, his everything. He never had, *didn't* have, time for relationships. He definitely didn't have what it took to keep a woman like her. Innocent and fragile, complex and defensive. He couldn't let her mess him up like this, couldn't let her—

The stinging peal of his watch fractured the moment with the same effect of a hammer swinging at the closed walls. He pulled himself away from the welcoming warmth of her body, frowning.

Natalie stiffened just as he clicked on the warning trigger he'd programmed into his cyber infrastructure.

The alert he'd put in himself took a few seconds to sink in.

A rogue bot program was loose in his network. Scouring every nook and cranny. Searching for something.

He looked up.

Guilt screamed from Natalie's stiff posture. She looked sexy and wrung out, mouth swollen, a pink mark on her neck courtesy of his teeth, dress rumpled.

"A rogue bot program is scouring through my personal security network, destroying each level of encryption like a deck of cards. I'm assuming that is you?"

That was why she'd been so restless and nervous all evening? Why she had…

He cursed so filthily that the air should have turned blue. "Was that—" he pointed to her disheveled dress, his mouth twisting "—to pacify me when I discovered what you'd been up to?"

Whatever color had filled her cheeks mere minutes ago fled, leaving her pale and shivering under the glare of the lights. But she bucked up, tilting her chin up, gathering that toughness she wore like an armor all around her again. Shutting him out. "Don't be nasty, Massimo. It doesn't come naturally to you."

He flinched. "Then what the hell am I supposed to think?"

Her arms went around her midriff. She looked lost, defensive, utterly enchanting. "I… I didn't exactly plan for…to throw myself at you tonight. I've been wound up all day, wondering where it would end. After that evening of—" her arm trembled as she pointed to the outside world "—pretending to be everything I'm not, of being near you and wanting you and not knowing what the hell is right and wrong—" she bit her lip and groaned "—something snapped inside me. I wanted to be reckless, and daring and just take what I wanted. You… God—" she pushed her hands through her hair "—only you do this to me.

"Really, if you use that incisive mind of yours, you'll realize that I don't have either the experience or the confidence to turn…this thing between us to my advantage. A pity that, because then I could've gotten myself out of this mess the moment you caught me."

His watch emitted another beep, jerking his attention back to the pressing matter. This time, it was an alert he'd programmed to go off when anything accessed a particular directory. The one that had files pinning Natalie to the security breach. This time, he wasn't surprised. He knew where her bot program was going.

"When did you go into the lab?" he asked, trying to sift through the anger and outrage and so many other emotions.

"This morning, when you were meeting with Leonardo.

And just before we left, again." Sweat beaded over her upper lip, a faint tension vibrating through her body. "That second alert means my program found those files, doesn't it? I saw the layers of encryption around that directory."

"You planned to destroy the proof?"

"Yes. Then I'd have my freedom."

"Brilliant as always."

She laughed, the sound edging into hysteria. Her fingers crept into her hair, tugged, and then she dropped them with a soft gasp. "All day, all night... I've been going crazy. When you said you'd let Leonardo handle the situation, I wondered..."

"What?"

"I wondered how long it'd be before you decided you'd been lenient enough with me. I was just waiting for him to turn me in." She swallowed and looked away. "I was terrified. I felt as if I'd lost everything all over again," she said, fear turning those beautiful eyes into wide pools. "I was determined to destroy all the files you have on me."

"What did you intend to do once you destroyed the files?" he said, something building in his chest.

"I was going to beg Greta's help and run far away from here. From you. She'd have helped me. She hates me."

"You had everything planned, didn't you?" He'd been expecting something like this from her. "The sheer nerve of you to hack into my network and let something like that loose...while you kiss me at the same time..."

"Sheer nerve? How about desperation? I'm sinking, Massimo. I don't know which man to trust and protect and which man to betray…terrified that I'll make the wrong decision."

"It's not hard to stay away from the man who's doing illegal things. Not hard to stay on the right side."

"Only a man born to privilege can be so absolute about right and wrong. A man who's never known hunger. A man who's never had to worry where he would sleep that night. I don't know why he's doing this, but he's not a monster.

"He saved me from a bully, from a bastard of a foster brother. He saved me from going to juvenile detention. He…he…for years, he looked out for me. He… caught me trying to steal his wallet and fed me a meal when I was starving.

"He found me a place to live, gave me money to get my own place. All these years, he never asked me for anything. He only gave, Massimo. He…said he saw something of himself in me. Years and years of favors.

"And when he asked me to do this one small thing of taking down BCS, wrapped it in lies I could swallow, I bought it willingly. I did him the favor. I… The second time, when he asked again, I could have said no. He wouldn't have pushed me. But I'd been caught in my own hubris, lured by the challenge of taking you on.

"So, no, I can't betray him. Even if I hate that he threw me into the middle of some awful vengeance scheme he's been cooking for who knows how long. Even if I hate that he's causing you…this much trouble. And I don't even hate him fully for involving me in this, because how could I?

"If not for him, I wouldn't have met you. If not for

him, I wouldn't have known what it was to want a man so much that I can't breathe. Can you imagine how twisted up I am in all of it?" She wiped the lone tear off her cheek, her chin setting into that stubborn tilt. "So the only rational thing I knew to do was to try to steal that proof before you sent me to jail.

"But... I couldn't. I just couldn't. All evening, I've been wondering if I've gone insane. Wondering if I'm really losing it."

Massimo felt as if she'd hit him in the solar plexus. Punch after punch solidly connecting, knocking the breath out of him. "What do you mean you couldn't?" Another damned peal from his watch.

"That bot program is only meant to locate my files. I... I couldn't bear it if you hated me. I couldn't bear to break your trust.

"But I had to break this impasse. So I went back and I tweaked the program to just locate the files. I meant to show you that I'm capable of saving myself, of betraying you, again, but I choose to not do it. To show you that I... I would never break your trust again, Massimo. Just please don't ask me anything more. Don't ask me for what I can't give."

So much she held on to, so fully, so completely she gave of her loyalty even under the harshest conditions. It wouldn't have cost her anything to give this man up. To look out for herself. And yet, she wouldn't... He didn't know whether to kiss her for her guts or to banish her out of his life for making everything so complicated.

He thought he knew her.

Dios mio, she'd told him enough about her background. He knew enough to understand that to survive in a harsh world, she'd become tough, and that she hated to be vulnerable in any way, that she was a wild thing that wrapped herself in layers of armor to protect herself…but this, for her to be willingly vulnerable to him, for her to give over her freedom, her security, into his hands, trusting that he'd do the right thing—the devastating result of that was in her eyes wild with fear, in her mouth that didn't stop trembling, in her body vibrating with tension.

This was ravaging her.

And yet, she'd done it.

To gain his trust.

The weight of her admission humbled Massimo, the emotional expectation beneath that decision…did he even deserve it? Did he want it?

She rubbed her eyes, smudging the mascara, ruining the makeup that he hadn't, leaving her still breathtakingly lovely, starkly beautiful. Eyes that had glazed over during her release filled with alarming tears. "I hate that you make me so weak. But I'm done fighting it."

The *swish-swish* of the elevator doors behind him revealed the stunned faces of Leonardo, and Greta. With Gisela and her father behind them. They'd been gone too long. *Maledizione*, the last thing he needed was the whole world to hear that his fake fiancée had been ready to leave him.

And still, Massimo couldn't find a mask to pull. Couldn't dig deep enough to care.

Let them think it was a lovers' quarrel. Let them see how crazy Natalie could drive him.

He pushed his hands through his hair and went to her, not wanting the world to see her like that. Not wanting anyone to see the vulnerability in her posture. Clasping her jaw, he tilted her face up to him. "What shall I do with you, *cara mia*?" Laughter burst through him and she stared at him, as if he'd lost his mind.

Had he? Would she leave with him with not even a semblance of control? It felt as if he had crossed some hitherto invisible line, had left safety and sanity behind. She'd dragged him into a new place, a place where he didn't know who he was anymore. Where emotions barreled through him.

He struggled under the weight of tenderness, of possessiveness, of deflated outrage. God, this woman… she stole the very breath from him. "You'll drive me insane before you're through with me," he said, before he kissed her hurt mouth. His lungs seemed to fill with air, his limbs infused with energy again, as she sank into the contact. He tasted her tears, her soft admission, her vulnerability. He held her tight, wanting to capture the essence of her.

"I… I'm tired, Massimo." She clung to him like a rag doll. All the fight and fury had deserted her. Her breath whispered over his jaw, her hands roving over his chest. "I'm tired of being tough. I'm tired of being pulled apart. I'm tired of worrying about my brother, about you, about the man who started all this. About everyone else when all I want is to…

"You…you're shredding me into so many pieces." Her fingers traced the bridge of his nose, his mouth, his chin, even the small scar on his temple.

The look in her eyes, longing and something more, arrested him. "With your kindness, and your charm, your laughter and your warnings. Your second chances. Your innate goodness. Your kisses. Your..." She looked down, dashing her gaze away. "But remember this, Massimo. When I could've freed myself from this dangerous game, when I could've protected myself—the only thing I know how to do—I chose instead to keep your trust.

"When I could've, *should've*, escaped, I chose to stay. With you."

CHAPTER TEN

MASSIMO STOOD IN the study that he and Leo used sometimes, a drink in his hand, his mind drifting from thought to thought, landing on the woman in the guest suite upstairs.

What would you do with me if I were all yours?

Maledizione, he couldn't forget that line or the vulnerability in her face when she'd said it. Still couldn't wrap his mind around what she'd done tonight.

He verbalized his frustrations into a pithy curse as he heard the door open and close behind him, knowing who it was.

Leo's laughter had such a shocking mirth to it that he turned. "I'm glad you think this is funny."

"I was just remembering Giuseppe's and Gisela's expressions earlier. I think you erased any doubt as to where your…interests lie, back in that elevator."

"And you've come to congratulate me about it?"

"Are congratulations in order? That didn't look like a fake engagement."

He scowled. "Cut to the chase, Leonardo."

"The way you spun it with Giuseppe—that the hacking attack and the security breach was something you had planned to find flaws in the system, that you brought her on for that express purpose—Silvio and I can use that same logic successfully to calm the board's considerable doubts and questions at the gala. Thanks to your quick thinking, we're in a good place.

"But it is imperative that we do something aggressive about stopping this…man, Massimo. Before we sign on with Giuseppe Fiore. Even a whiff of scandal like this again—"

"Could ruin that project before it even begins," Massimo finished, giving voice to his greatest fear.

Relief filled Leo's eyes and Massimo laughed. "You think I do not see the risks? You think I'm that far gone?"

Leo shrugged. "Women, and relationships for that matter, this family, this legacy, have never been an important part of your life before, Massimo. Even with your mama, you hardened yourself, letting her go so completely. You…simply decided Silvio had tortured her enough, decided that you were a weakness dragging her down. I'm not quite sure I'd have been able to do that. You decided you'd focus on your career, your ambition, you decided you would conquer whatever demons you had, and you did it. For a decade, I've watched you work crazy hours, go from strength to strength."

Massimo frowned. He had never looked at it quite that way.

"But with Natalie, you went rogue, completely off script, from the minute you met her.

"Honestly, I don't know what to think. I can't help but think maybe you've lost your edge for…this."

His brother's perceptiveness rendered Massimo so shocked that he could barely muster a response. "I haven't."

"And maybe you need to be told that it's not a—"

"Leonardo! All I will say is that yes, Natalie disarms me like no one else."

"I have to admit that to prove to you that she could steal it but not actually do it... I still don't feel comfortable that she could so easily ruin everything you're working toward, but I have to admire her guts. I can admit to seeing the lure she holds for you."

Massimo's problem was that he was beginning to admire a lot more than just her guts. Was beginning to lose his control, his path. "The Fiore contract is still my first priority, Leo."

"Bene." Leo nodded. And his vote of confidence meant something to Massimo. "I will not waste time and energy worrying over you, then. Greta and Silvio are far too much already. What did you find out from her?"

Massimo looked away. He'd never been so conflicted in his life. And he didn't like it one bit that she did this to him.

He walked across the study, taking in the expansive room that had been the seat of his father's power when he had ruled most of Milan as the CEO of Brunetti Finances.

Usually, he preferred to not step foot inside here, since all the memories he had of this room were of being summoned by Silvio at all hours while he was recovering from another asthma attack or a fright induced by an approaching one or when he had failed to exhibit great athleticism or when he saved a kitten. There had been countless things, and then being shouted at that he needed to let go of his mama and grow up and be a man.

That she was coddling him too much. That she was making him soft and spoiled.

That he would never be man enough or strong enough or ruthless enough like Leonardo. Never good enough to be a Brunetti.

Today it seemed like the two parts of him—one with an unending thirst to prove himself to Silvio and Leo, the entire world and to himself, and the second, the weak boy whose mother had tried so hard to teach him right from wrong, who had told him to define himself in a different way, his own way, who tried to negate the harmful narrative his father had perpetuated in the house for so long—clashed violently.

Dios mio, his mother had put up with Silvio for so long for Massimo's sake. She had tried so hard to stop Massimo from thinking that he had to be cruel and ruthless to be powerful and successful. In the end, she'd found love with another man, forced to choose between a new life and Massimo.

Massimo had bid her goodbye happily at the age of fifteen, desperate for her to find a little happiness, desperate for her to stop sacrificing herself for him. But there had been selfishness on his part, too. He'd been determined to prove that he could survive without her shielding him from reality.

And he had succeeded beyond his wildest dreams.

He had carved his own path, found his own empire. His

cyber security business had infused much needed capital into other branches of Brunetti Finances, a dynastic multigenerational financial institution, when it had been limping along on its last leg. His brainchild, BCS, was the only reason they stood irresolute and unshakable today when most of Europe—and Italy, in particular—were floundering and falling into financial crises.

And when they signed this hundred-billion-euro contract with Giuseppe Fiore…there would be no looking back.

Yes, Leonardo was right that they still needed to find the man who was targeting them. But no, he didn't need to hold Natalie's freedom over her head to achieve it.

It was not a weakness to grant her her freedom. Not a weakness to achieve his goal, realize his ambition without crushing the one powerless person in all this. Not a weakness to grant her that desperate sense of control she needed over her life.

I chose you, Massimo.

That constant knot in his gut slowly relented, a sense of rightness settling his breath.

He saw the study with new eyes. Leonardo had decided to redecorate the space. The transformation had been fantastic—it had gone from a cloying, ghastly room with so-called precious antiques to an open space with contemporary art and clean lines.

Greta had put up a dirty, vicious fight carping on about legacies and dynasties but Leo had shut her up. But it had been a new direction for Brunetti Finances, and even better, it had been a new direction for the Brunetti brothers to take the company, their legacy.

"She told me enough about this man to give us a trail to follow. A money trail. He transferred her money when she turned eighteen so that she could get off the streets. I'll dig down to the exact dates once I get out of here. All we need is to trace her bank account to see where the deposits came from."

"And his name?" Leo prompted, clearly not satisfied with what Massimo gave him.

"There isn't one."

"Massimo, you have to make her tell you—"

"*Nessuno!* I will not," he said softly, "coerce her or threaten her with imprisonment. That's my final decision. She has too much stake in this now, Leo. I need her by my side to keep Gisela in line, with Giuseppe so close to signing. I need her to work by my side on the security designs. You saw how impressed Giuseppe's CTO was with her tonight."

"You're basing a lot of important things—things we've worked years for—on the fact that you trust her. Her loyalty—"

"Is not something that can be bought or forced. The way Silvio got things done, we swore we would be different. We swore we'd build our fortunes the right way.

"Natalie will be an incredible asset to not just BCS but Brunetti Finances in the long run.

"It's plain, pure business sense."

Leo finally nodded. "*Bene.* As long as you're sure that's your guiding principle, I will follow your lead."

"It is. It has to be," Massimo reiterated to an empty room long after Leonardo left.

* * *

Natalie let the stylist use her like a fashion doll. She let the makeup artist pull and prick her scalp, straighten her hair to an inch of its life, probably burning away most of it, in the process of making her good enough to be the fake fiancée of the Brunetti scion.

A week since the disastrous and most spectacular night of her life, Massimo hadn't decided her fate. Still. Despite her throwing herself at his mercy. Despite puking her guts about how much he was coming to mean to her. Worse, her emotional outburst seemed to have only pushed him away. Filled the space between them with an awkward kind of tension she couldn't disrupt.

Excusing themselves to a curious audience, he had dragged her home that night. Warning her to do nothing for once, if she knew what was good for her. Closeted himself in the lab. The next morning, he'd shown up at her door again at the crack of dawn, like clockwork. For a whole foolish minute, she'd hoped he'd come for… personal reasons.

Nope, the workaholic that he was, it had been back to business. At least he hadn't revoked her electronic access to his lab. He had made her sign what felt like a hundred contracts, officially bringing her on the payroll for the Fiore contract, including confidentiality agreements and waivers and whatnot.

Making it clear that she wasn't going anywhere, anytime soon.

Once she'd started thinking straight again and not out of a desperation born of lust and longing, she realized Massimo couldn't simply tell the world that his fiancée was a criminal or send her to jail.

There was the little matter of their fake engagement. She couldn't contest the fact that he needed her—at least as his fiancée—to keep Gisela in line. Especially since it looked like Giuseppe had been more than impressed with Massimo's initial design and, with his reassurance about bringing Natalie on, more than ready to sign off the contract to BCS.

Now, he had officially tied her to that contract, too, by bringing her on as a consultant. Her future was secure. Not just secure. Better than ever before. Because Massimo Brunetti was a generous employer. She could put away so much for Frankie's college. She could save for a future.

He'd even let her Skype with Frankie. More than once. Forced her to introduce him, too, since he kept hanging around during the call.

He hadn't asked her a single question again about Vincenzo.

All this generosity was beginning to choke her since he didn't even…really look at her anymore. She much preferred his accusation that she'd been trying to distract him while she deceived him rather than this polite distance, this courteous withdrawal. He didn't laugh with her, he shared no horrible hacker jokes that he found on the internet, he didn't tease her into kissing him.

A week since that night—the night her body had come alive in his hands so violently that when she went to bed every night, she closed her eyes and touched herself, trying to recall his warmth and scent and his desire. But her fingers were poor substitutes to his wickedly clever ones. So she tossed and turned, feeling a restless hunger after being cooped up with him in the lab for the whole day. Being near him, touching him accidentally, breathing the scent of him until he was a part of her.

And now this engagement party… It wasn't too much of a reach to think Greta was doing this to punish her.

She sighed when the stylist finally finished with her hair and the two too-cheerful assistants plonked a full-length mirror in front of her.

Despite her glum mood, Natalie's attention stirred.

Her hair straightened into a silky curtain fell past her shoulder, giving her the sleek sophistication she'd always wished she possessed. The white strapless gown that had been chosen for her fell a few inches past her knees, its beauty lying in the clean, classic A-line cut. It hugged her small breasts, clinging to the dip and rise of her waist and hips, ending in a big ruffle at the end, a beautiful feminine touch to contrast the severe cut of the bodice.

Pale gold powder accentuated her cheekbones and brow, and a glossy pink lipstick subtly enhanced her lush mouth. This look was night and day different from the one last week. Of course, that afternoon, she'd explicitly asked Alessandra for the kind of look that arrested Massimo's gaze, in her desperation to be worthy of him.

Tonight, about to be presented to Milan's Who's Who on the Lake Como estate, which was the home turf for the Brunettis, the stylists seemed to have been instructed that she needed to look classy, elegant. Instead of resenting the high-handed approach, Natalie decided to embrace it. Really, she had disadvantages enough when it came to Massimo without falling into a pit of insecurities about how she looked.

She'd just pushed her feet into bright pink pumps the stylist said would add a pop of color to her outfit when Massimo walked in.

His gaze swept over her, a soft smile playing around his mouth. The first one in a week. "You look…beautiful, *bella*."

In a black tux that highlighted his wide shoulders and lean waist, he looked absolutely gorgeous. Divine. "You look good enough to eat," she retorted, and he laughed.

"Well, it's the truth."

"I'm glad the true you hasn't been buried beneath all the primping, *cara mia*."

And just like that, her heart fell right into his clutches. God, she was really tired of the impasse between them. "Massimo, can we please not…"

She closed her mouth when he pulled out a small velvet box. Without asking her, he reached for her hand and pushed the princess-cut diamond ring in white gold onto her ring finger. "I… I have been remiss about that. Appearances must be maintained, *sì*?"

Natalie folded her lips inward, stalling the pinch of hurt. "Of course," she added, pasting on a fake smile. This was getting harder day by day. "Appearances are the most important. Even for fake Brunettis," she couldn't help adding.

He smiled, as if he were delighted by her snark. "Your bot program was brilliant. I didn't think you could take down the encryption around that directory, truly."

"Your ego is not dented?"

His mouth twitched. "You know me better than that, Natalie. I've never asked you to hide what you are capable of, from me. I never would."

Feeling like a fake of the worst kind, she nodded. What would he do, however, if he knew the extent to which she'd used those capabilities to survive her life, she wanted to say. She swallowed the question, struggled to push away the niggle of shame. Her past was just that. The past.

And then he was pulling out something else from his pocket, and Natalie's breath stuttered in her chest. Palm up with it in the center, he looked at her. "I went the old-school route. I saved it on a flash drive. And the directory you found… I've scrubbed it permanently."

Her knees threatened to buckle from under her. "What?"

"The files are gone. The trail is scrubbed. This is the only remaining copy of everything I put together to find you."

"You're giving it to me," she finished lamely, her throat aching, tears gathering like a storm.

Only a nod.

"With no conditions?"

"*Sì*. You'll never have to worry about ending up in jail. As long as you don't do anything criminal again, that is," he said, the corner of his mouth tilted up, a glimmer of that teasing Massimo in his eyes.

She swallowed, but the boulder-size lump in her throat wouldn't budge. She wanted to grab the flash drive and run away. Far from this man she couldn't seem to dislodge from under her skin. Far, far away from her own heart's stupid longings.

"Why are you doing this?"

"I'm trusting you. Isn't that what that stunt was about?"

"It is. And I'm glad. But…where do you and I stand, Massimo?"

The warmth disappeared from his eyes. "We still have an agreement. You're clever enough to understand that you can't just up and leave. Not now when you're an official employee of BCS. Not when Giuseppe is ready to sign on the dotted line. Having heard of her unstable reputation, I shouldn't have messed with Gisela. Even if she knew the rules of the game. I'm afraid she's fixated on me."

She nodded, agreeing completely. "I won't let you down. I promise. I'll play the part of your perfect fiancée as if I was born for this role. I'll be nice and sweet to your family and in public—"

He laughed so loudly that his brother and Greta looked up from the foyer where the first guests were beginning to arrive. "Do you know the meaning of the words *nice* and *sweet*, Natalie?"

"I do," she replied, basking in the warmth of his laughter. She loved it when he was like this—smiles and teasing—and…she loved that he understood her so well, and that he…

A wave of shock rolled over her.

No, she didn't.

She couldn't love him.

How could she, when she didn't even know what it meant? When all she'd ever known was survival?

No.

She was mistaking gratitude for a deeper emotion. It couldn't be love—could it?—when the very prospect of it terrified her to her soul. When the very idea of giving him so much power over her threatened to break her out in hives. She trusted him more than she did anyone in the world and she wanted him. That was it.

"Leonardo thinks I'm foolish to take such a gamble on you again. Don't make me lose face with him, *sì*?"

"Sì." When he turned to leave, she grabbed his arm. "Wait, Massimo."

He folded his hands. *"Sì?"*

She turned the engagement ring over and over, feeling its weight on her soul. "What about you and me?"

"There is no you and me. There should never have been, you were right.

"I'm still recovering from a stupid mistake I made by tangling with Gisela. Even knowing that I was going to do business with her father, even knowing that she… had the reputation of being wild and unstable.

"And you—" his gaze drank her face in "—you've never even been with a man before. The last thing I need is to make another misstep like that, with you of all people. You're far too—"

"If you say I'm innocent, I'll hate you. Don't take away the power of my choice from me."

"We belong in different worlds. Want different things

in life. I will not do anything that will rock the boat now, now that BCS is going to handle a hundred-billion-euro contract any day. Now that you're an important, moving part of the company.

"I can't afford to blur the lines in this relationship."

If he had thrown her into jail, Natalie would have been less shocked. A sense of falling, with no safety net, claimed her chest.

"Shall we go?" he said, offering his hand, and she nodded. Her other hand closed over the flash drive.

She was free, finally. For once in her life, she was getting a break. More than she deserved. And yet, freedom had never felt so costly to her emotions.

Tears stung at the back of her eyes but she held them back. Just. A cold that was absolute took hold over her.

He'd given her everything she'd asked for and more.

Gave her back her freedom.

Given her a secure future.

And yet, this…this distance he imposed, this calculation in his eyes that she was a weakness he couldn't afford, this was a rejection. Like he'd given her everything and yet taken away the most important thing from her.

Him.

He'd taken himself away. From her.

For a woman who'd built her whole life being self-sufficient, trusting no one, why did it feel like such an aching loss? Why did it hurt so much?

And was she prepared to let him do it? She'd always had to fight for what she had, worked hard just to keep her head above water. Now when she was faced with losing something truly important, was she prepared to let it go so easily? Was she really going to let Massimo push her away?

No. No she wasn't.

She wanted Massimo. And she was going to fight for him.

CHAPTER ELEVEN

PREDAWN PITCH-BLACKNESS WAS a thick blanket Natalie had to wade through as she made her way to Massimo's room.

She was done living in caution, done safeguarding her heart. She wanted, craved, that excitement. She wanted whatever pleasure Massimo could give her. She wanted, even if only for a few days, a few months, whatever time, to be the woman who brought out the wicked, wild side of the tech billionaire.

Except from the moment he had put the ring on her finger and dealt her that rejection several days ago, he hadn't looked at her once with that desire in his eyes. Not once had he been tempted among all the evenings they'd spent in each other's company. Not once had his polite mask slipped.

Enough was enough!

The marble was smooth and cold under her bare feet. Having learned his punishing schedule by rote— billionaires really worked the longest hours—she'd de- cided to just…show up at his door. She heard a sound from within just as she raised her hand to knock and decided against it.

Why give him a chance to reject her again?

Slowly, she turned the knob and stepped into the lounge. A small lamp at his desk illuminated the sprawling sofas and the contemporary art on the walls. She rubbed her feet on a thick rug, relishing the warmth of it. The sound came again—a cross between a moan and a growl, sending shivers down her spine. A thousand thoughts flashed through her mind—did he have a woman in there? Had he already moved on? God, was he *refueling*? If he was, she'd…throttle him, the unfeeling brute!

She didn't even have to barge into his bedroom for he had left the door open. Tugging the cashmere shawl she'd wrapped around her shoulders tighter, she stepped in.

The massive golden shaded lamps on both sides of the even more massive bed emitted a soft yellow light. Papers and electronic devices lay scattered on the nightstand. A gray suede headboard framed most of the wall. Dark gray bedcovers were rolled away. A white towel dangled off the end of the bed. And at the foot of the bed, leaning against it, stood Massimo.

Stark naked.

Head thrown back.

Breath coming out in harsh inhales and exhales.

Neck muscles corded tight.

Defined chest muscles gleaming with dampness. Falling and rising.

Abdomen so tightly packed that she wanted to run her tongue along it and see if he was really that tight.

Thighs rock hard and clenched, dotted with hair.

And his hand wrapped around his...erection. Even from the distance she could see the corded tightness of his wrist, fingers wrapped tight, and the head of his erection visible above his fist every time he moved his grip up and down with a grunt that seemed to claw up from his chest.

Heat licked up every inch of her stinging skin instantly. Every inch of her body reacted to the gloriously aroused naked man in front of her, reveling in sexual abandon. Her breasts turned achy and heavy, nipples knotted points rubbing against her T-shirt. And there was that wetness at her sex, readying her for him. Her skin felt as if it were two sizes too small for her feverish muscles.

Her breath left her lungs in an audible gush like a balloon deflating. And then she struggled to get more air in because there was none left in the room. She gasped under the overload of sensation.

Massimo's head jerked down, breath shallow. His gray gaze pinned hers to the spot, pupils dilated. He frowned, his hand coming away from his erection, which bobbed up against his taut belly. With shaking fingers, he rubbed his face with his other hand. And then looked at her again with an intensity that seared her. Twin slashes of color climbed up under his olive skin.

Had he realized she was there, not in his imagination? Oh, God, please let it be her that he'd been imagining...

"You shouldn't be here, *cara mia*," he said, husky

desire making his voice low and raspy. Even his words seemed to ping on her skin, overheating her.

"Did I ever give you the impression that I'd abide by your rules?"

"No," he said, leaning that tight butt against the bed, jutting those lean hips up, so confident and comfortable in his nudity. So utterly, irresistibly male. "If you did, it would solve a lot of problems for me."

"I want to be here. All week, I've been trying to muster the courage to walk in here. All evening, I readied myself for you. I've plucked and waxed and bleached and shaved and peeled and massaged..."

He cursed. Then laughed. Then shoved his fingers through his hair. "You don't have to change yourself, in any way. I want you just the way you are, with an insanity that for the first time in my life even work won't do it for me. I think of you all the time...which is hard enough because you're there by my side 24/7."

Simple truth. No games. "Then why pull away from me?"

His gaze swept over her face, her neck, her sleeveless tee and her shorts, her thighs, her legs. "I swore to myself a long time ago, even if I forget it from time to time, that I would never be the kind of man who hurts... fragile things. You're...breakable, Natalie. I'll use you, and then break you, before I discard you. I couldn't face myself then."

She'd never seen him like this—so desperately hungry, such stark need in his eyes. So much desire that her first instinct was that he would drown her in it, make her lose herself, and running away was probably the best thing. But she refused to listen to that flight instinct. No, she would stay. She wanted to stay. She wanted to drown in him. "I don't need you to save me from you or from myself, Massimo. I don't want a hero. I've never asked for one. I've always saved myself. Found another way, another path.

"I want a man to show me all the stuff I've missed out on because I was so afraid for so long. I want a man who will help me live, experience, feel. For however long we want it to be.

"I want you, flesh and blood, like this, desperate for me. Out of control. Stripped to the core. Because that's how I stand before you."

Each second of the silence that ensued let panic loose in her head. He was too honorable, too much of a protector, to take her. Not unless she drove him to it. She needed to be the aggressor, at least until he got his hands on her. Then all bets were off. She knew. She knew how desperately he wanted her.

She took a few steps toward him, not quite touching distance. The jut of his shoulders, those rock-hard thighs—every muscle in him clenched tight.

"Were you thinking of me?" she asked, licking her tongue, wondering why her mouth felt so dry. "Please tell me you were thinking of me and not another woman. Because I'd have to hunt her down and kill her."

A dark smile split his mouth, a beacon of light in the darkness. A flash of that wicked, wild Massimo that she adored. A glimpse of the man she was falling for, fast. But there was only exhilaration right now in her veins. Only anticipation, excitement.

"Morning, noon and night, I think of you. I go to bed thinking of you. I wake up hard thinking of you. You in that gold dress, a goddess teasing and taunting me. You in that yellow bikini, like a sunflower in a field of frost. You in that white cocktail gown looking so demure and classy and calm and nice and sweet."

"Are you insinuating I'm not classy?" She pouted, taking another step. She was walking into a lion's den, she had no doubt. A willing sacrifice. And yet, she'd never felt so alive. So present. So in touch with herself. All of her.

His gaze swept over her with a warmth that was just as arousing as the desire. That made her feel safe. Secure. That made her want to throw herself headlong into this. "You're tart, and down to earth and loud and snarky and wild and…you're a summer storm, *mia Natalie*."

Happiness was a fountain spurting in her chest, overflowing to every empty space within her, filling her with a warmth she always felt when she thought of him. She touched him with her gaze—that high forehead, sharp cheekbones, aristocratic nose, carved mouth, the tendons in his neck, the sparse sprinkling of hair on his pectorals, the defined lines of his abdomen, and his… his erection thickened and lengthened under her gaze, and her panties were soaked. A growl fell from his mouth, filling her veins.

She rubbed a hand over her nape and then over her breasts, aching all over. "Did it work?"

"What, *cara mia*?"

"Thinking of me, and doing that...did it relieve your...ache?"

Thick lashes flickered down and then up again. His shrug brought her gaze back to the jut of his shoulders. Tense. Taut. Really, his body was like a treasure, and she didn't know where to look or what to touch. "*Sì*. For short periods of time."

"It didn't for me."

A rough thrust of his fingers through his hair. An infinitesimal tremble of his chest. Her words were getting to him. A jolt of power filled her. "What?" he breathed.

"I...tried it, too. Touching myself, trying to find relief.

"After that night when you made me..." She swallowed at the devilish cast to his features. The need he couldn't hide. "Every night, when I go to bed after spending all day with you, I feel so restless. As if I were a prisoner in my own skin. I'd shower, remembering your smiles and your teasing and your hunger that night, and the strokes of your fingers... By the time I got out of the shower, I'd be thrumming with need. I'd get into bed and touch myself.

"One hand cupping my breast and one hand, delving into my... On and on... I'd be wet and I tried to... But I...just ended up making it worse." She swept a hand over her breasts and belly and his gaze followed her movements, like a hungry hawk circling. "I... If you're not going to take me to bed, at least maybe you can give me some pointers?" She bit her lower lip and took another step. Another soft growl from his chest.

He didn't look like the suave, charming tech billionaire that had people eating out of his hands. No, he looked savage and rough, like the lowest denominator of himself.

"You want me to show you how to get yourself off?" Disbelief couldn't puncture the desperation.

She shrugged.

He cursed and laughed and cursed again. His powerful body rumbled with the force of it. "*Cristo*, you were sent to torture me."

"You look like you've had a lot of practice. I could just—" she turned around and saw the chaise longue "—sit there, y'know, and you could stand there, and we could—"

"Only since you came into my life, I've felt this madness, this constant fever. I'm like…a goddamned teenager, needing to jerk off every few hours."

"I've never been so jealous of a damn hand. That hand."

She pressed her palm onto his abdomen and he growled, arresting her wrist in his hand. He was like a slab of damp heat and delicious hardness under her fingers and all she wanted to do was roll around in his heat, in his scent, until he was imprinted on her very skin.

"*Dio en cielo*, Natalie. If I do this, one night won't be enough."

Lifting her gaze, she held his. Saw the last thin thread of control separating them. "Who said anything about one night?" One more push and he would be hers. She pulled her hand away from his grip, and ran a finger over his length and moaned softly. How could he get even harder and bigger? "Shall I go down on my knees?"

His eyes gleamed. With need. Danced at her offer. He was tempted. *Hallelujah!* "You've got guts, bluffing your way through this, daring me with your tempting offers. How do you know you'll like it?"

"Will *you* like it?"

"*Si.* It's all I can think of when I want to shut you up. When you argue with me. When you use your damned loyalty against me."

"Then I'm sure I'll like it, too."

When he simply gazed at her, she gave voice to her innermost desire. Pressing her forehead to his chest, she licked his skin. Tasted the essence of the man. Salt and musk and pure Massimo. "Please, Massimo.

"I... I want to be here, Massimo. Only here. With you, in that bed. Under you. Over you. Any which way you want. I can't sleep, I can't think straight...even my dreams are restless and leave me aching and wanting. You're the only man that has ever made me want to live. Live for myself. Experience everything life has to give. Risk myself. To laugh, cry, howl, plead."

To love with such abandon that would have terrified her before... She didn't say it.

It was the simple, incredible truth. Like the sky was blue and the earth was green and the world was a harsh and lonely place but also joyful and full of wonders if only one had the courage to step out and reach for them.

Love and its demands and its constrictions and its expectations had no place here tonight. Or maybe ever, with Massimo. And that was a price she was more than willing to pay to own a part of this incredible man, even if for a little time.

His fingers sank into her hair, and he tugged so hard that her scalp prickled. That, too, added to the surfeit of sensations beating her down. She felt his mouth at her temple, his other hand running in mesmerizing circles over her back and buttocks and hips, and he was tugging her T-shirt up, up and away, over her head, and pulling her into him, and suddenly, her bare breasts were pressed against his damp chest, her nipples dragging against the wall of his muscles, and they were both sinking and drowning and gasping at how good it felt.

Her hand slid back to his solid erection.

"No," he said abruptly, practically screaming the word into the darkness that enveloped them. As if he needed to control and corral this boundless want between them. "No, you can't touch me, not yet, *cara mia*. Not tonight. If you do, it will be over before we even begin and there's so many things I want to do with you before I'm pounding into you. So, no, no touching me. Get it?"

Natalie could barely form coherent thought, her brain too busy processing the deluge of novel sensations pouring into her. All she could do was press her mouth into his shoulder and dig her teeth in. Holding on to him.

Rough hands on her buttocks picked her up, pushing her thighs shamelessly wide, her feet on top of his buttocks, his hip bones digging into her fleshy thighs, until her sex was notched oh-so-snugly against his shaft.

"*Merda*, you're dripping wet. Is this for me, *cara mia*?"

"All for you. All I…feel is for you, Massimo," she whispered, and then she took his mouth the way she wanted to. Thrusting her tongue into the warm cavern of his mouth. Pressing it against his, retreating when he tried to catch her, sucking on his tip, tugging at his lip with her teeth, drawing blood, licking at that spot, until he was shuddering and shaking and pulling her down, down, down into a vortex of sensation that swallowed her up.

And then he was turning them and rocking her into that massive bed, giving her the friction she needed exactly where she needed it. His shaft pressed and slid and glided and rubbed against her clit and she caught on to his rhythm and was pushing herself into him just as he rocked his hips… Her swollen nipples scraped against the rough hair on his chest, his mouth buried in her neck told her in explicit terms how he was going to take her bold offer one day and put his shaft in the warmth of her mouth, and Natalie was drowning as pinpricks of sensation poured out from her neck, her mouth, her breasts, her belly, pulling and tightening and building into concentric circles in her lower belly, and she was sobbing, clawing her nails into his damp back, demanding he give her more…

Instead, he pulled away. Brought her down shaking from the cusp of pleasure and Natalie railed at him with her fists. Afraid that he'd leave her unfulfilled. Afraid that this was another dream she was going to wake up from. Afraid that she'd go through her entire life and not know his touch.

"Shh…*tesoro*," he whispered at her temple. "Look

at me, Natalie. I'm going nowhere. I couldn't even if a thousand hands tried to rip me away. I couldn't leave if my breath depended on it."

Her bottom met a cloud of soft sheets, and when she opened her eyes, he was looming over her, sweat coating his skin, smelling like man and heat and sex and belonging. He kissed her bruised lips, so softly, so sweetly, so tenderly. "You trust me, *si*?"

"I do. Like I never have another man. I…" She rubbed her fingers over his swollen lip, the tiny cut she'd given him. She searched for something light to puncture the dam of emotion building up in her chest. "I took a risk on you, Massimo. Pay it up, *per favore, caro mio*."

He nodded, a wicked light in his gray eyes. "Put your hands above your head. Clutch the sheets if you need to. But don't touch me, *si*?"

She nodded, biting her lower lip. And watched him. Anticipation built up slowly this time. His mouth drew down on the pulse at her neck, while his hands plumped her breasts, readying her. She arched like a bow when he tugged a nipple into his mouth and suckled, a little roughly, building that fever in her veins. That tension in her pelvis again. "*Cristo*, you will come like this if I continue, won't you?"

She nodded, and of course he released her breast. "And you're going to be thorough and detail-oriented, aren't you?"

With a roguish smile, he continued the foray of his mouth down her body. Licked maddening circles around her belly button. Natalie was panting again, gasping for breath as he separated the folds of her sex with his fingers.

She felt him pulling in a deep breath, pulling the scent of her arousal into him. Heard his pithy, foul curse breathe into her skin. Felt the tremble in his shoulders. And then his fingers were at her clit again. Stroking, swiping.

"Is this what you did?" he whispered against the crease of her thigh. "Is this how you pleasured yourself?"

She opened her mouth and swallowed air. Somehow she managed to say, "But it's nothing like when you touch me." God, nothing and no one in the entire world was going to feel like Massimo ever again.

Then his mouth replaced his fingers and his fingers were inside her and all her fears vanished under the onslaught of the sharp sensations. "Like this?" he whispered, weaving some new magic.

"Or like this," while he explored her, learning, and gave her the key to her own body.

And he was licking at her tight bundle and hooking his finger until he touched some magical spot that sparked fierce pleasure in her pelvis. On and on, again and again, until she was nothing but pure sensation. And when he pulled his mouth and fingers up and away from her, Natalie followed him with her hips, sobbing and begging. And then he tugged at her clit with his teeth.

Pleasure threw her apart into so many pieces, fracturing her, tossing her, and he continued crooning against her sex and she kept coming, tears flowing out of her eyes, and she dug her fingers into his hair, because she was afraid he had broken her apart and she would fly away. She writhed on the sheets as the waves slowed and ebbed, whispering his name over and over again.

She was lost in a sea of pleasure. She was lost to this man, forever.

When he climbed onto the bed and he pulled her into his arms, his thighs cradling her hips, she folded like a deck of cards, shivering and shaking. He was a fortress of warmth and safety at her back. She rubbed her nose in his bicep, loving the smell of him. When he stretched his arm to reach into the nightstand, she stopped him. Looked at him over her shoulder.

"I'm on the pill. Alessandra took me to a pharmacy."

He raised a brow, the ghost of a smile shimmering around his mouth, and she blushed. How could she blush when he'd put her body and her emotions through a ringer?

"I wanted to be prepared." She kissed his chin. Nipped it with her teeth. Felt his erection like a hot brand against her. She wriggled in his lap and his fingers dug into her hips with a curse, hard enough to leave bruises. So she did it more. And he groaned. "I was going to have you, come what may. If you didn't know already, I'm a determined woman."

"That you are," he said, turning her to face him. "I'm clean." A flash of white teeth. "You can tunnel into my network and see the medical certificate."

She shook her head, smiling. If only she could somehow tunnel her way into his heart, too… She pushed damp tendrils of hair away from his face, burying fear deep inside. "I don't have to."

"It will hurt," he said, his features severe. His strokes on her face gentle. "I… I've never made love to a virgin so you need to tell me if it's too much. If it hurts too much. If you just want a breather or want to stop completely. I'll stop, *cara mia*. Anytime."

"I want this, with you. Only you."

He touched his forehead to hers, and gave her the softest, sweetest kiss. Even inexperienced about men, Natalie had a feeling he was bracing himself for it. Gathering his control. Because she knew him. She knew he'd never forgive himself if he hurt her.

Muscles that seemed to have turned into so much blubber firmed up as he pulled her up into his lap, pushing her thighs indecently wider. His kisses shut rational thought away, going from soft and tender to hungry and urgent in a matter of seconds.

She felt his erection hard and demanding against her belly. Threw her head back as his hands plumped her breasts, rolled her nipples. He whispered endearments into her skin, tasted every dip and rise. Told her how much he'd dreamed of her like this—completely his.

Slowly, with infinite patience, with skillful touches, he aroused her spent body until she was shivering again, and there was wetness at her sex. His clever, wicked fingers played with her, working her over, building her to a fine fever, cranking her on and on. Already he knew her body so well. Better than she did. And she wanted to chase that mindless high again. Fall down hard from it into his solid arms. Again and again, until she didn't know where she began and he ended.

And then he lifted her, murmuring soothing, soft words, and she looked down, refusing to miss anything, and he took his shaft in hand and drenched himself in her wetness and then he was there at the entrance to her body and his hands on her shoulders were pushing her down, and with one smooth, hard thrust, he was inside her.

She cried at the sharp, unending pinch of pain, tugging at his hair while he buried his face in her neck. His breathing was loud and hot and his big body was so tight as if he were spending an enormous amount of control to stay still. "*Merda*, you're like a glove. So good, so…" He looked at her and cursed. "I'm hurting you, *si*?"

She nodded. And he kissed her softly. Butterfly kisses at her cheekbone. The tip of her nose. The corner of her mouth. Beneath her ear. At the juncture where her neck met her shoulders. "It's okay, *cara mia*. Just… just hold on. We'll stay like this. As long as you need. Or I'll pull out and we'll try again some—"

"No." He was like a hot, hard poker inside her and she never wanted to move or let go. And he was frozen like one of those marble statues littered all over his damned estate, so rigid and hard and taut and tense around her. Inside her.

Natalie pushed back with her fingers on the jut of his shoulders and gasped when even the small movement sent a sharp pinch through her pelvis again but she desperately wanted to look into his eyes, at this man who had stolen her heart. The invasion of his shaft and the pain of their joining, and the comedown from her orgasm—everything was conspiring, pushing her toward tears, pushing her toward hiding away from this moment, toward an emotional climax just as powerful and even more dangerous.

For the one thing she couldn't do was throw herself open even more. Not when she wanted a lot more of this intimacy with him.

So, she kissed his temple, tasted the sweat of his skin. She wrapped her arms around his shoulders, needing the glide of his bare skin against hers, needing the closeness. Needing the scent of him deep inside her. "Tell me, please, tell me what to do. I want this to be good for you. I want…"

He caught the tear falling down her cheek, and kissed her temple as if she were the most precious thing he'd ever held. "Good, *cara mia*? If it got any better, I'd die from the overload."

He rotated his hips slightly, softly, and Natalie gasped. Laughing. "That wasn't so bad."

When he laughed, she bit his lip.

"No, that was fantastic. Great. Do it again. Please, Massimo."

Massimo thought he'd die if he didn't start moving soon. Pressure knotted up in his balls, tingled in his lower spine. And yet, he'd rather die than hurt her. "Are you sure?"

"Yes. Hundred percent. Move. Now."

And she demanded that he move inside her like she

demanded everything else of him. Boldly. Honestly. Courageously.

Holding her hips, Massimo pulled her up a little. And brought her down just as he thrust his hips. The friction was amazing. The pleasure she gave him indescribable. Another thrust. Another stroke. He stilled to delay his climax rushing at him. "Listen to our bodies, *cara mia,*" he whispered, laughing, when she bumped into him on a downward stroke. "Listen to your instincts. Try swiveling your hips, moving this way and that. Just…find your rhythm with me."

"So less bumping and grinding, and color by numbers and more instinct, Massimo?"

"Yes, more instinct. Less numbers. Especially when it is this good," he said, giving her a wink.

She laughed, pushing her hair away from her face, thrusting her breasts in his face. This time, she met him thrust to thrust, in perfect synchronicity, creating magic.

Cheeks pink, brow dampened, hair a wild cloud around her face, eyes glazed with passion, mouth swollen, she was the most breathtakingly beautiful thing he'd ever seen. She was passion and enthusiasm and joy and he felt as if he was drowning in her.

He pushed her onto the bed and covered her, increasing the tempo of his thrusts, all but mindless in the pursuit of his own climax. Picking her up by the hips, he angled her so that his abdomen rubbed over the top of her sex every time he retreated and she was sobbing again, writhing and digging her teeth into his bicep as she splintered, and Massimo followed her.

Two hard, swift thrusts and he came in a rush of heat and lightning. Afterward, laughter followed, for only his brave little hacker could make him laugh in such a moment by shouting, "Hell, yeah, that was awesome, Massimo. How soon can you go again?"

He let his hard body cover hers completely for a few seconds, needing this closeness with his lover for the first time in his life. Needing to steal away something from her, for himself.

Maybe he wouldn't ever be able to offer her what she deserved from a man. But he was determined to never hurt her, to never dull the spark that fired up his brave, little hacker.

CHAPTER TWELVE

"How much longer are you going to avoid me?"

"What?" Massimo said, loosening the knot of his tie. He shrugged off his suit jacket and leaned against his bed, just…drinking in the sight of her.

A weak spring sun dappled her in golden light as Natalie stood in front of the French windows that framed his bedroom. She'd given up fighting to subdue her hair today apparently because it was loosely tied in a ponytail at her nape.

Today, she wore a pristine white sleeveless shirt that showcased her toned arms and flowy pants that sat low on her waist, leaving a slash of that taut abdomen he had licked just last night, on his way to other important things, bare for his gaze. The diamond pendant on a delicate gold chain he'd bought for her gleamed on her skin.

It had taken him three arguments, two days and one…session of persuading her with his fingers and mouth and tongue before she'd accepted the gift. Before confiding that it was the only piece of jewelry she'd ever owned.

And then, of course, being the extremely competitive

woman that she was, she had proceeded to pay him back in return for his wicked persuasion. Her hair tickling his thighs, her mouth laughing and licking and wrapped around his arousal, she'd driven him to the most powerful climax of his life. Leaving him stripped to the soul.

Just thinking of it, of her, of her unflinching, unending desire to know all of him, to learn all of him—he was turned on simply by looking at her, his arousal a throbbing need in his trousers.

"Something's wrong, Massimo. You and I both know it."

He willed his body to focus on her words. His mind to maneuver the minefield of confrontation that they'd both been pushing away, desperate to not test this... thing between them just yet. Or was he the only one who thought like that? "I'm not used to sharing every small thing that occupies my mind," he bluffed.

Something was wrong with him, *sì*. But he didn't know what or how to fix it.

Her chin fell and she nodded. "But this is important enough that you distanced yourself from me. You do that when you have a design problem, did you know that?

"You swim endlessly...you box in the gym...you avoid looking at the problem until it works itself out in your head. I know you, Massimo. Better than you think."

Three and a half weeks since the night she'd snuck into his room and proceeded to blow his mind. His hunger for her only seemed to increase the more he touched her, the more he kissed her, the more he basked in her laughter and her quick wit and her affection.

She brought out the best in him, and yet, she brought out the worst in him, too.

He wouldn't have realized how seamlessly she seemed to work herself into his life until that meeting that had wrecked the bliss of long, drawn-out nights amid silky sheets and the exhilarating rush of pitting his mind against hers during the day.

Natalie was a woman unlike any he'd ever known, for he had a feeling he would never know all of her. Possess all of her. Just when he thought he did…another facet of her was revealed.

Even at a recent meeting with Giuseppe Fiore's CTO, his first instinct had been to defend her, to protect her from even a whiff of accusation, to storm out of that meeting until he could process it on his own.

"Your fiancée is a common thief."

"That association could cost you, Massimo, your reputation at least, if not this contract, if it gets out."

Since Giuseppe's CTO was a friend of his, Massimo had convinced him to put it aside. Massimo had used an invaluable business connection to vouch for Natalie. Created a debt for himself in a cutthroat business world.

A small thing but an unprecedented thing. A fissure in the line he drew between his ambitions and his feelings. Blurring the lines between what he wanted to be and what he was.

Dios mio, she complicated everything with her truths, and her lies and her dares and her kisses, and he needed to get a handle on this and her. Fast.

He'd screwed the chance of keeping things between them separate—professional and personal. He'd blurred all the lines between them from the moment he'd seen her walk out of that club.

When he'd decided she would be the perfect foil to discourage Gisela Fiore.

When he'd decided she would be an asset to BCS. When he'd brought her on board to work on the Fiore project. He'd lost his mind from moment one. Lost all caution and discretion and common sense that had made him such a world-renowned success before thirty.

She'd fought him from the beginning, on every arrogant assumption of his, at every decree he had laid down, even his short-lived honor. She'd told him clearly, point-blank, that she didn't give her trust easily. She'd told him, again and again, that her loyalty had to be earned and couldn't be bought. That her heart, she'd lived with it under lock and key for so long.

So, this was on him. And yet, he also wanted to blame her. To use this as a reason to push her away. To…stop this madness before it deepened and someone really got hurt.

Her—she would be the one who was hurt in the end.

"I've been busy," he fibbed. "This project is taking everything I have."

"I know you're busy. I'm in there with you most of the time. But this is not just work stress. This is not you tuning everything else out to untangle an analytical problem.

"You've been freezing me out for a week. I don't know why or what I did. You won't…look at me. You won't smile. You…don't talk to me in the lab. You… come to me in the middle of the night and make love to me, but by morning…you're back to behaving the same way again.

"It's almost as if you're…ashamed to converse with me outside of bed."

"You're being ridiculous," he said, an inane response to her perceptive gauntlet.

"No, I'm not. You didn't even tell me how exceptionally clever my design was for the bank's interactive portals. If nothing else, I count on you to tell me how brilliant I am on a regular basis, Massimo."

That irreverence, that honest but baffled admission— it was a balm to his masculine ego. Which the woman had the disconcerting knack of knocking off balance with a regularity. At least she was in this madness as much as he was.

"Are you done with me, with us, Massimo? Is that it? Do you want to move on?" Vulnerability in her voice even as she stubbornly tilted her chin up. "Because if you are, just…tell me."

"Nessuno," Massimo answered automatically, speaking his instinct before even processing that question.

"I can take it. I told you I don't need—"

"Fiore's CTO, Franco, summoned me last week to tell me he'd discovered that you had a juvenile record. As part of the routine background checks they do on every member of this team.

"For a *financial crime*, Natalie!

"Do you realize what that does to BCS's image? After everything we've had to put up with over the last few months? After all the fires I've been putting out? Now, when we're so close to that contract?

"*Cristo*, Natalie, is it true?"

All color fled her cheeks. She looked down at her hands and then up at him, her heart in her eyes.

Something in his chest deflated, as if he'd been expecting her to deny it. Call it just an accusation. Demand that he listen to the truth. What a coward he was that he couldn't face her truth. Couldn't face the power she already had over him.

"Yes, it was when I was fourteen."

His curse rang in the room.

But she didn't flinch. "I transferred some money from my foster father's bank account to his daughter's. He was a bully and she offered me two hundred dollars for it…" She shrugged, as if it didn't matter. "I had already learned how to break most security designs. I… The cyber investigator—it took him forever to pin me down for it. The judge sentenced me to community service, and a warning, and sealed those records. Those should have been sealed records. It was a juvenile offense. Before I met *him*. Before he persuaded me that I couldn't continue like that… I didn't know right from wrong, Massimo. All I knew was survival."

Tears filled her eyes and she looked away from him. Her body bowed as she stared out the window, and all he wanted was to pull her into his arms and hold her tight. To tell her that no one would ever push her to that ever again. That she'd never be so alone in the world.

Instead, he stayed where he was, watching her, willing this desperate need inside him to calm, willing rationality to take over again.

How had he picked the one woman who with every breath, every word, jeopardized his goals? Why didn't he just push her away, now that he knew the truth? Why couldn't he say yes, this association was too costly for him?

Why didn't he just draw the line here, now?

Every rational instinct he possessed urged him to do it. Better late than never. They could just be colleagues and still live under the same roof. He'd done it so many times before.

And yet, he stood, every muscle frozen.

Slowly, her shoulders straightened. He saw her dash away the tears with a rough gesture.

"You should have told me."

She turned back to him, her eyes shining with pride. "I didn't realize I was supposed to tell you every part of my unsavory life."

He rubbed a hand over his forehead, hating that he made her so defensive. "This is a hundred-billion-euro security project for a finance empire. All of us will come under the microscope. I can't keep covering for you. You should—"

She pushed away from the wall. "Did it ever occur to you that I was too ashamed to tell you? Or that it's not a part of my life I want to advertise to you when I'm begging you to not send me to jail? Or should I tell you when you already think I'm deceitful and low class and—"

He pulled her into his arms, incapable of not touching her.

She didn't come easily. Her fists came at his chest, her body shuddered; she jerked in his embrace, but he held fast. Willing her to trust him. Consigning the war between his mind and his heart to hell.

"Let me go, Massimo."

"Calm down, *cara mia*. I just…"

"You what?" She pushed her hair away from her face, brown eyes shooting daggers at him. "You are ashamed of associating with me. You're already calculating damage control. You're…"

He flicked his lashes down, afraid of what else she'd discover that he didn't even know himself. Those eyes taunted him before she laughed. A sad sound filled with bitterness and pain. Pain he was causing her. Doing the one thing he swore he wouldn't do.

"Wow, you're no better than one of those supercomputers of yours, calculating gains and losses per transaction, per every interaction you have with me, huh?"

"Stop, Natalie. I told you to give me space. I was going to work it out. You're the one who pushed me into this…discussion.

"I've already asked the project manager to take you off the team for now. You just need to lay low until Fiore signs, that's all. It won't go any higher up than this. His CTO will arrest it there. Especially since those are sealed records.

"But we can't risk you being on the project. We can't… If there's anything else I should know…"

"How about I sleep separately for a while, too? How about you come back to me when this is done?

"Is that what you've been finding so hard to say?

Too bad you tied yourself to me in front of your whole bloody world, *si*? Too bad you can't just throw me out of your life as easily as you can cut me out of the project?"

"Natalie, you know what this project means to me."

"You… My past, who I've been, who I am, is a liability to you. You…you weigh everything in life to see whether it serves your ambition or not. You weigh people around you in terms of assets and liabilities.

"I'm a liability. I'll always be a liability to you.

"But I refuse to be ashamed of who I am and what I've done in the past to survive."

Natalie let the hot water pound at her, washing away the sweat and grime of her workout. Wash away the tears that should have dried up a long time ago.

With a groan, she pressed her head into the cold tile. The worst part was that, despite her defiant words to him, she did feel ashamed. Wished she could change things she couldn't undo now.

And even worse was the feeling that she wasn't good for him. Good for his image. Good for the Massimo Brunetti who was going to take not only Milan but Italy by a storm with his innovative cyber security design for Fiore Worldwide Banks.

That she would never be good enough.

She rinsed off the soap, lethargy and tiredness crawling into her muscles. And she felt him standing outside the shower before she heard him, the scent of him calling her.

"Can I come in?" he asked softly, though he was already partly inside the open gap in the marble-tiled shower, his hair catching on water drops, the front of his unbuttoned shirt more than half-damp.

She turned, angling her body away from his gaze. She wasn't really a shy person but she couldn't brazen it out, either. Neither did it stop her skin from tingling in a million places. Waiting for his touch. For her body to tighten and clench and loosen in anticipation of the drugging pleasure he could give. And gave frequently and generously and at every chance they got.

God, he'd even persuaded her onto the table in his lab while they'd been working late one night. Dropped to his knees and tucked his head between her thighs and now she couldn't walk into that lab without blushing and heating up.

And here she was again, after that argument, standing there naked, letting him look her over, going weak at her knees wondering where he would take this… If she wasn't a pushover, she didn't know one. "I'm almost done."

A small smile played around his lips. "I don't really want to be in there if you get out." He leaned against the wall, pulled up his knee and watched her. As if his goal in life was to watch her bathe. "You have a little soap you need to wash off. There. Under your right breast. Where you have that mole. Where you…"

Her breasts were heavier, her nipples tight buds begging for his attention, her sex wet and willing by the time Natalie mustered enough senses to understand his game. "It's not fair. We had a fight and sex doesn't fix it. Even the fantastic sex you give."

His smile vanished, though the warmth of his

gaze didn't. "*Sì*. We did have a fight. And maybe you could've been more honest—" he raised his hands in surrender when she opened her mouth "—if I had been more thorough about the scope and reach of this project. If I hadn't backed you into a corner.

"I brought you on, so the mistake is mine.

"But it doesn't mean, never did it mean, that I don't want you here. In my room. In my lab. In my life.

"I'm trying to make this work, *cara mia*. And no, I've not been and never will be ashamed of what you had to do to survive. You're right. I can't imagine what it must have been like to be that girl who had no one, the girl who had to make herself so tough." He cupped her cheek, his thumb pushing away the tears that trailed down them, his voice so infinitely tender. His lips were warm and familiar against hers. "Meet me halfway, *tesoro*. Just…let me get through this milestone. I need you here. I want you here."

And just like that, with easy charm and sincere words, he made mincemeat of her anger and her hurt and her defenses. He hadn't apologized, really, for putting that contract above her. He didn't even think of it that way.

He was far from admitting, even to himself, how much he cared about her, much less to her.

But he made accommodations for her in his life. And he let her know how much he wanted her. It was more than Natalie had expected of him, entering into this relationship. God, he'd never lied to her where his priorities lay.

She pushed her wet hair away from her face and nodded.

He inclined his head.

The antagonism in the air shimmered away, instantly replaced by hunger and heat.

"I missed you," he said, his head completely in the water now. "Yesterday. In my bed. I didn't sleep well."

She was tempted to say she had slept soundly. But they didn't play games with each other. Not when it came to this. Here, there was only truth. Utter truth. "I didn't, either."

"Say no if you don't want to do it in the shower, *cara mia*."

"Can I say yes?" she said, reaching for his shirt and pulling it out, seeking the hard, warm male skin.

He smiled and pulled her to him. And took her with a devouring hunger that filled all the empty places inside of her. He told her with his kiss, his touch, his hard, hungry caresses what he would never say in words. His arms caged her, as if he meant to never let her go, his belt buckle digging into her belly. "I want to be inside you, now. Please, Natalie."

"Now is good. Now is always good with you. Take what you need, Massimo," she said, and somehow, they managed to undo his trousers, push the wet fabric past his lean hips, and she wrapped her legs around him, and he rubbed at her clit to check she was ready and then he was inside her.

Natalie threw her head back, feeling him all over inside her, in this position. He was in her breath and in her blood and in her heart. And any fear that she was heading for a heartbreak of epic proportions melted away under the onslaught of sensation when he flicked his tongue over her nipple.

She rocked into his thrust when he turned her to the wall and swirled his hips. Her breasts bounced and scraped against his chest, and she felt the tension coiling in her belly and when he pressed her against the cold tile and brought her hand to her clit and smiled wickedly, she massaged the swollen bundle.

And when he took her mouth, hard and fast, all the while rocking into her with short, swift thrusts, Natalie let go of all the fears and doubts and let herself be washed in him, in the pleasure he wrought in her, in the magic they created together.

A week later, Natalie clicked on the encrypted email that was sitting at the top of her in-box on the tablet Massimo let her use, her heart racing, threatening to rip out of her chest. She'd instinctively reached for her tablet, wanting to see if Frankie had replied to the stupid meme she'd sent him about cats.

Massimo lay on his chest with his arm over her midriff, still asleep.

Meet me tomorrow. One p.m. at Piazza del Duomo. V.

Her heart thumped, her pulse racing with fear. She exited out of the program quickly, spending two more minutes to clear out the history, erasing every inch of her account from the hard drive itself.

Vincenzo was here? In Milan? What did he want with her?

She wanted to throw up at the very idea of lying to Massimo again. At the very thought of deceiving him.

If she told him, he would forbid her to go. He would... tell Leonardo, and God knows what Leo would do.

But how could she just...not go?

What if this was her chance to convince Vincenzo to stop this crazy agenda? To find out why he was doing this in the first place? What if she could solve this problem, once and for all, for Massimo and effect some kind of peace between him, Leonardo and Vincenzo?

Then she would be more than a liability. Then she'd be worthy of his respect; she'd maybe even be worthy of him.

CHAPTER THIRTEEN

PIAZZA DEL DUOMO, Milan's main, spacious city square, was bursting to the brim with tourists and locals as Natalie walked in on Tuesday afternoon. Pausing, she looked up at the massive facade of the Cathedral of Milan. The architecture was magnificent and she desperately wished she could have a carefree day with Massimo.

On the other side was the world famous La Scala Theater he'd promised to take her to soon.

The cobblestones clicked beneath her black pumps, the air filled with the decadent scents of chocolate and coffee, friends and lovers calling out to each other, buzzing with energy. The constant knot in her belly she'd been walking around with since yesterday tightened when she spotted the dark head, sitting at a table outside a café.

Palm flat on her belly, she walked toward the table just as Vincenzo looked up. Almost severe in their sharpness, his features lent him an austere beauty that arrested more than one woman walking by. Dressed in a blue dress shirt and black tailored trousers, he was the epitome of masculine appeal.

"Come, Natalie," he said in that deep, bass voice she had known for so long. When she didn't move, except to stare at his outstretched hand, a dark smile played around his lips. "Come, little cat," he said again cajolingly, using that little moniker he'd always used. "I won't bite, *cara mia*. You know that."

Natalie shook her head and took his hand. He clutched her shoulders and studied her face. Bent his head and kissed her cheek. And slowly, his arm wrapped around her shoulders, pulling her to him. He was the same man who had done her a thousand favors, the same man who had kept her safe, helped her make a life for herself.

Natalie went into his arms, even though she felt as if she was betraying the man who'd again and again given her his trust, his loyalty, and earned hers in return.

There was something so familiar about Vincenzo—the scent of the cigar and his aqua cologne—that she calmed. "You're well?" he breathed the question over her head. "You weren't mistreated?"

She felt the tension in him dissolve when she nodded. He wasn't a monster. Not the man who worried about an orphan he'd saved years ago. "You know I can watch out for myself."

"I had to remind myself of your strength every day. There was no way to get in touch with you. I went to see Frankie and he said you'd called him and told him you were leaving the country for a friend's wedding. He was super excited for you."

Natalie's heart crawled up to her chest. "You saw him? He's good?"

"He's doing great."

"Thank you," she whispered.

"How are you doing?"

"I'm fine, Vincenzo. I've been…good, too."

He stared at her questioningly, but nodded.

He pulled a chair for her and then settled into the next one. When the waiter inquired, he ordered two coffees for them, telling the waiter to make hers extra sweet and extra milky, with a distasteful scrunch of his nose. Natalie laughed, and tucked an errant curl away.

His gaze arrested on the diamond on her finger, and she hastily dropped her hand.

"What I heard through the grapevine is true?" The warmth didn't quite leave his eyes but there was something else.

Natalie opened her mouth and then closed it. She wanted to ask him so many questions: how long had he been in Milan, in Italy, what was he planning and why. But she curbed her curiosity. She didn't want to get in the middle of this. Not after today. Also from everything she'd learned in the last two months, he was a master chess player, moving pieces back and forth, ten moves ahead of everyone else. "It's a fake engagement. Too convoluted to explain."

"Massimo shouldn't be trusted. None of them should be. Using people is in their blood—"

"You're the last man who should lecture about using others. You—"

"I never forced you. You could have said no at any time."

"You knew I wouldn't. You manipulated me… I could've gone to jail."

"I trusted you to look after yourself. I would have been there, within the hour. You know that."

Natalie wanted to say no, she didn't. But seeing him again like this, she couldn't. How could she convey all the complex emotion twisted around this man to Massimo? How could she convince him that Massimo didn't deserve what he was doing? "This is such a…mess. Please, tell me you're done."

He shook his head and her heart dropped. "Stay out of it, *cara mia*."

"You dropped me in the middle of it."

"You shouldn't have gotten caught. You're supposed to be brilliant."

"I got caught because Massimo's just as brilliant as I am. But he's also kind, and funny and charming and… He could have sent me to jail and he didn't, even when I refused to give him your name."

"I wouldn't have held it against you. You're a survivor, Natalie, just like I am."

"Loyalty means something to me. Massimo's a good man, Vincenzo." She reached for his hands, as he'd done to her long ago. Hoping to get through. Hoping to stop this before more people got hurt. "Whatever you're doing, he doesn't deserve your hatred."

He studied her slender hands in his, squeezed them and then slowly released each finger. Slowly but surely shutting the door in her face. When he looked up at her, there was such dark emotion swirling in the depths of his gray eyes. "This started long before Massimo became the financial force behind Brunetti Finances, Inc. But he's a part of it. They all are. For years, they perpetuated what…" He looked away, as if to control himself. "This won't stop because you like him. This won't stop until…"

He stood up, and Natalie's hopes dashed into dust.

She looked up at him in his black suit jacket and tailored trousers and expensive haircut, and the way he stood…her heart ached for whatever drove him to this. "Until what, Vincenzo? How much more hurt will you cause before you stop?"

He offered her his hand and Natalie stood up, their coffees untouched.

Suddenly, he felt like a stranger. Like he'd never shown her his true self. She wanted to run back to Massimo, and beg him to fix the whole sorry mess. And he would, she knew it.

He would at least listen.

Vincenzo took her elbow as they stepped away from the table. "Return with me. My jet's waiting."

Natalie stared back, stunned. "With you? What? Where?"

"I don't want to leave you here, with them. Not after today, and not after… I want you far from here. Back in the States. Safe."

His words pelted Natalie's skin like small cold stones. She pushed away from his touch. "Vincenzo, please, put an end to this."

"This doesn't involve you. I'd hate to hurt you any more."

"It involves the man I trust and if you do this… I can't

keep you a secret anymore. I won't. He's earned my loyalty. I work for BCS now. On a dollar-huge project for Fiore Worldwide Banks. I—"

"He won't win that contract."

Natalie felt as if he had punched her in the gut, as easily as he smiled at her. "Yes, he will. I designed it with him. I won't let you steal this away from him. I won't let you hurt him."

And it would, she knew for sure.

Massimo prized that contract above his relationships. Above everything else.

"Massimo Brunetti is a genius who treats women no better than his father did. In the end, he is his father's son. Prestige, family name, power, that's all that matters to them. He will delete you as he does yesterday's technology as soon as you become irrelevant. Come away, Natalie. I don't want this on my soul."

"Do you have a soul?" she whispered at him, and he flinched. "You can't escape the consequences." Tears filled her eyes. "I thought I could fix this, appeal to you. But I don't know who you are.

"Don't contact me. Don't try to save me. Just…stay away, Vincenzo."

The *tap-tap* of her pumps on the marble floor cranked up the panic running through her as Natalie walked into the sitting lounge. She came to a stumbling halt as four sets of gazes swiveled to her with a wide range of expressions.

The Brunettis were out in force.

She took a few more steps into the lounge, her heart

beating so fast that she was afraid it would rip out of her chest. Massimo stood all the way at the back of the vast room, his back to her, the tension in his shoulders making her own tighter.

Her belly somersaulted with fear.

Did he know she'd gone to meet Vincenzo? How?

Leonardo seemed the most relaxed, sitting in an armchair, Italian-loafered ankle crossed over the other knee, swiping something on his cell phone. There wasn't the usual cynical amusement or contempt in his dark gaze. Just plain curiosity. As if he were a predator deciding whether he wanted to rip her apart now or later.

She walked past him to where Massimo stood with his back to her.

"Massimo? What happened?"

He turned, and the fury in those eyes stopped Natalie in her tracks. The dark emotion touched all of him—those perceptive eyes, the bridge of his nose, that mouth that could curve with such wicked laughter—making him look so severe, so much like one of those portraits she'd seen in that long hall, contemptuous and arrogant.

The Brunetti aristocracy of so many generations that he thought he didn't belong with. Men steeped in power and prestige and cruelty.

Dread knotted in her chest that she had to force herself to breathe first, but it was centered on what Vincenzo had let loose this time. "Massimo, why are you guys still here? I thought you were meeting the Fiore team for the official signing—"

"I canceled the meeting."

"You canceled the meeting? Why?"

"Our security design for FWB was stolen from the network server and published on the Dark Net. A half hour before our meeting." His body bristled with unspent fury. "A year's worth of work out there for any hacker to go through, to target the banks. Thousands of customers' financial information would have been in jeopardy. I had to disclose the hacking attack to them.

"The intricately detailed triggers you executed… I knew the plans were being stolen the minute someone tunneled in."

"Wait? I don't understand. That design was brilliant. The security layers literally incorruptible. You saw what I built…you went over that design with me with a fine-tooth comb. It can't just—"

"I thought so, too. But then it's not so hard if you handed over the blueprints to all the layers, is it? Or, say, if you logged into the server and created a tunnel for them to access it?"

Natalie stared at him, her mouth opening with an inaudible gasp, her brain processing his accusation over and over again. Because he couldn't be saying what he was saying, could he? "You're blaming this on me?" Her throat was achy and full of tears and she looked around as if she could gather strength from something or someone, but instead only saw the accusation now in their eyes.

"You think I… I gave them access to the server? I let them in? I helped steal plans I toiled over with you for the last few weeks?"

"It happened when you returned from your secret meeting and accessed the server for the plans."

Vincenzo had played her so well. "You can't... I did log on to it. I accessed the plans, yes, but only to make sure the security layer was tight. Something he said made me realize they might not be as safe as we thought. You can't think—"

"Something he said? Or something he asked you to do? Is it that much of a stretch for me to believe that you followed the instructions the man gave you when you met him this afternoon?"

Accusation after accusation and Natalie had nothing to fight them with. She'd been so foolish. God, if only she hadn't gone to meet Vincenzo this afternoon, if only she...

"Massimo, I didn't. I didn't betray you. I know how this looks, okay? But I—"

"Who did you meet this afternoon?" he finally said. As if she were a stranger. As if he hadn't made love to her this morning.

"Vincenzo. His name is Vincenzo Cavalli." His name dropped into the silence with the same effect as if a meteor had crashed through the roof, into the room. Natalie saw Leo coming alert, clicking away on his phone, but nothing could tear her gaze away from the cynicism in Massimo's own gaze.

"There, I said his name."

Massimo smirked, and she hated everything about it. "Did he give you permission now that he has done irrevocable damage to us?"

"He sent me an encrypted email, asking me to meet him, and I—"

"Then why didn't you tell me? *Cristo*, you were in

bed with me when you got that email, weren't you? You smiled at me, you kissed me, and you lied to my face. You promised your loyalty was mine. You promised…" He thrust his fingers through his hair roughly, shaking. "You could have told me he contacted you. You could have told me where to find him. You could have solved this problem for us. But no…instead, you decided to protect him. Instead, you chose him.

"I trusted you. I let myself feel…but in the end you picked him. You jeopardized everything I've worked for, all these years. Leave, Natalie."

"Don't say that. Please, Massimo, I want to help you fix this. I can help—"

"Get out. Get out before I—"

"Before what, Massimo?" she shouted back, tired of his accusations, tired of being afraid. Tired of…the emptiness that waited if he kicked her out. "What would you do to me?"

"Call the *polizia* on you. Have you arrested for corporate espionage, for breaking a hundred confidentiality agreements, for selling your loyalty. I don't think you stopped being a thief."

If he had slapped her, Natalie would've been less shocked. Less hurt. Pain came at her in huge, rollicking waves, twisting her belly, knocking her out at her knees. "How… That's so unfair. You can't… I can't believe you would throw that at me? Knowing why I did it. Knowing… I trusted you to understand. To…"

He searched her face, studied the tears running down her cheeks. Maybe, for a second, he even softened. Natalie saw the familiar Massimo, the Massimo she loved with her whole heart, in his eyes before he shut it down. Before he shut that part down. Or maybe it was all her foolish hope. Her blinders still on when it came to him. "You didn't trust me with it, either, *cara mia*. You hid it. And you defended yourself, as you always do, when it came to my notice."

"Massimo, think it through before——" Leo chimed in.

"Now you support her, Leo?" Massimo's voice was cutting, so full of bitterness. "When all along you've been asking me to throw her out? When she's proved you and Silvio right? When my allowing her into all this, when my trusting her, trusting my emotions, is what brought us to this?"

With one last look at her, Leonardo walked out.

Massimo tucked his hands into his pockets, every inch that ruthless, powerful stranger who had cornered her that first night. "This is my fault. All mine.

"From the moment you came into my life, you never told me the truth.

"Why should I not believe that you engineered this? Why should I not believe that when I realized you were a liability...you jumped back to his side, you looked out for yourself once again?"

It was over, Natalie knew then. He wouldn't believe her. He had decided to not believe her. He had decided to finish this.

He had decided, maybe even before this, that she wasn't good for him, that he was done. And nothing she said would change his mind.

Her tears, her begging, nothing would dent that resolve she saw in his eyes.

Nothing… She wiped away her tears, anger rescuing her from the pit of self-pity and pain. Anger made her straighten her shoulders. Anger made her aggressive, see clearly. Anger made her realize how worthless she'd thought of herself when it came to him.

Anger made her realize how she'd strived to become worthy of him, how she'd foolishly assumed that he'd love her if she wasn't a liability anymore. She was done. God, she was so done with him, with thinking that she was less than him. "This is so convenient for you, isn't it?"

"Convenient?" he said, sneering. "You ruined a project that I've been working toward for a decade. You ruined my chance to—"

"To what? To prove to your father that you're not the sick runt he calls you still? To prove that you're better than Leonardo? To join those heartless, arrogant, bloated with power ancestors that are hanging on that damned wall?

"Your chance to prove to yourself that you're a Brunetti through and through—cruel and power-hungry and looking for any excuse to push away anyone who cares about you?"

"You've no idea."

"Of course I do. This project means everything to you. *I was there.* But…it is also such a good reason to push me away, too.

"Look in your heart and tell me you truly believe that I sold you out to him? This is not about me. This is about you.

"Because you feel something for me, too. A weakness that could weigh you down. Because I was becoming a liability to your goddamned reputation, your pursuit of billions, your ambition with my petty theft record. A liability to what you think Massimo Brunetti should be.

"Anything's better than examining what you feel for me. Anything's better than letting yourself love me. Anything's better than becoming what your father thinks you are.

"Because Brunetti men don't have weaknesses. Because Brunetti men are monsters.

"You act like you're better than them all but…you're the worst of them. You know better and you still cling to it. There's a little good in you and you kill it every chance you get.

"I fell in love with you. I was twisting myself up in knots that I wasn't good enough for you…but you're the one who doesn't deserve me. You're not the man I thought you were.

"Congratulations, Massimo. At least there will never be a doubt in your mind that you're a Brunetti, after all."

CHAPTER FOURTEEN

MASSIMO STARED OUT the window of his office at Brunetti Towers in the financial district of Milan, not really seeing the noisy crowds of tourists and locals.

The city's financial pulse—something he had always felt so strongly, something he'd strived to be part of for so many years, left him feeling nothing but emptiness. The villa, his flat in Navigli, even his lab—his lab, which had always been his sanctuary... Guilt haunted him, consumed him, ate through him.

Leo had probed and pushed and, in the end, given up. It wasn't as if BCS would die without him at the helm for a week. Vincenzo Cavalli could raze BCS to the ground for all Massimo cared.

He hadn't eaten or worked or slept in so many days. In the two weeks since he had thrown his dirty accusations at Natalie.

She'd been right.

He'd behaved worse than his father or Leonardo. He had always thought himself as better, prided himself that his mother raised him with different values, had assumed that when the right woman came along—

someone with class, and sophistication, and someone who understood that her place would always be second to his ambition—he would treat her well.

For all his arrogance and ambition, instead he'd found a woman who was fire and passion and love. When push had come to shove, he had proven himself to be worse.

The first day when he'd discovered that Vincenzo had hired a consortium of hackers to leak the security designs, using Natalie's past hacker activity as the key, he'd made a hundred excuses for his behavior.

She had been the gateway for them to steal the plans. He had never been taught how to process his feelings for a woman, especially such a complex one. She had come into his life at the wrong time. Part of it was her fault because she had gone to see Vincenzo behind his back…on and on and on.

He had prioritized the wrong thing in life. Looking for ways to end the one thing that made him look deep into himself, to reach for something he might not be capable of.

He was a Brunetti man who courted power, prestige and billions because he'd been terrified that if he wasn't the most powerful of them all, then he was nothing.

And yet, she had found something in him to like. To love, even.

"I fell in love with you," she had thrown at him, so full of pain, her eyes big and bright, bowed by his cruel words. But not broken.

Because she was right. He was the worst of the Brunettis, after all. He was the one not worthy of her.

She had survived with her heart whole, and courageous.

And if it took him the rest of his life, he'd spend it making himself worthy of her.

After numerous calls from his secretary and Leonardo poking his head into his office all of four times for an urgent meeting, Massimo forced himself to move.

He owed Giuseppe the courtesy of showing his face, even if the association they had both sought was a pile of ash. Pushing his gray suit jacket on, he ran a hand over his jaw.

Cristo, he must look like he'd been living under the green moss under the crappiest rock after his trip to New York and back to Milan in the space of thirty-six hours. Exhausted, he couldn't sleep because he hadn't found her. He'd even made a trip to see her little brother but Frankie hadn't heard from her except the usual, weekly check-in call.

Where the hell was she? Had she gone back to Vincenzo, knowing now that Massimo didn't deserve her?

Nauseated by his thoughts, he walked into the conference room and grabbed a bottle of water.

Giuseppe and Leo sat on the opposite sides of the long conference table with Franco next to Giuseppe and... *Natalie next to Leo*.

His heart thumped so hard against his rib cage that Massimo dropped the bottle of water. It hit the carpeted floor with a soft thump, rolling away with a swish. And he had the most ridiculous notion that it was his heart and he wanted to groan and laugh and share it with her, but he had hurt her with his cruel words.

Perversely, he'd never been so cruel to anyone else in his life, only the woman he loved. If that didn't tell him everything that was wrong with him...

He wanted to tell her he had all the time in the world to listen to her now but only silence was left. She'd taken joy and light with her.

Dressed in a white dress shirt that hugged her slender frame and black trousers, and hair—*Dios mio*, that wavy, thick hair, bunched into a sophisticated knot at the top of her head—she looked like composure, and sophistication, and brilliance and beauty and heart, all combined into a complex woman.

The woman he adored with every breath in him. The woman he'd go down on his knees for. The woman who could strip him to his soul with one look, one word, one kiss.

The woman who refused to shift her gaze from the laptop screen in front of her and spare him a look. The woman who was even now digging those misaligned front teeth into her lower lip.

"Massimo, take your seat," Leo said. Massimo covered the distance to Natalie, his chest such a tight knot that it was a miracle he could breathe. The scent of her, so familiar, made him shake.

Somehow, he kept his head as Leo began the meeting and Franco asked questions about the recent leak of the security designs while he made copious notes, and in between, there was Natalie, pulling up schematics for a new multilayer security design on the projector, addressing Giuseppe's and Franco's questions, and Massimo went from dumb disbelief to utter amazement.

She had come up with a new set of security designs? She'd been working with Leonardo? Giuseppe—who apparently appreciated Massimo's proactive backing out of the contract because of the security leak, whose CTO had been smart enough to recognize Natalie's unusual talent—had persuaded his board to give BCS another chance.

Natalie's frantic, almost feverish movements in collecting her laptop, her handbag.

He moved his body into her space and she stilled. "I've been to New York to see you. I've seen Frankie." When she turned her stunned gaze at him, he nodded. "He's good. He's excited to see you soon."

"Thanks, but I'll see him in a day. I've tried to repay any damage I've done to the project. You have it, Massimo, everything you ever wanted."

She hitched her bag over her shoulder, calmly dismissed Massimo and moved to Leonardo. There was no spark in her, no fight, no laughter, no joy. Just a... pale imitation.

"Thank you for letting me fix this. I'd prefer to work from home if you still want me on it. If you arrange for a ride to the airport—"

"You're not going anywhere," Massimo bit out.

"Massimo—"

Fury burned through him as he met Leo's gaze. "You know I've been going mad trying to find her."

Leo shrugged. "That day, you weren't in a place where you'd hear a word I said. No chance for rational talk. You persuaded me that she was brilliant. I saw no reason to not use her. Later, after I convinced her to fix it, her condition was that I not tell you."

Had she written him off completely? Had he lost her before he had realized what he'd had?

Leo closed the door behind him. When Natalie moved to follow his brother, Massimo waylaid her, trapping her between the table and his body.

"Let me go."

"*No!* Tell me why you helped." He wanted to touch her so desperately, more than he needed his next breath.

"Because that project meant something to me. Being on a team that created cutting-edge technology, being on a team with you and Leonardo and all those men and women, discussing strategies with you, building something real out of all those years of dreams…it meant something to me.

"More than money. More than the power or prestige of it. More than…" She looked away. "All my life, I've never been a part of a community like that. I wanted to finish what I'd started."

"Then stay. See it through."

"I can't stay near you."

He placed his hands over her shoulders, bracing himself against the waves of pain crashing through him. "Natalie *mia*, will you please look at me?"

He fell for her all over again when she leveled those beautiful eyes at him and gazed steadily.

"Where do I start, *cara mia*?"

"There's nothing to start, Massimo. Nothing to say…"

He clasped her jaw with his hand, his heart bursting with all the things he wanted to say. "First, I beg for your forgiveness, *tesoro*. Please, Natalie, if you ever thought that there was something worth knowing in me, loving in me, please, *cara mia*, you will stay a minute and you will listen, *sì*?"

She looked up at him then, meeting him square in the eye. Gaze filled with tears. "You shamed me. You… You gave me everything…everything I never asked for, everything I never expected to have in life. Everything I had never even dreamed of…and in one moment, one moment, you took it all away, Massimo.

"I've never felt so alone. More alone than that night when my dad didn't return. To not have known you would have been okay.

"But to know you and love you and love the best of you and then…" She looked down, and her tears poured onto her chest, dampening her white shirt. Massimo pulled her into his arms, unable to bear her pain, hating that he'd done this to her. "You made me doubt myself. As if I was less. As if I didn't deserve you. I only went to him to talk about—"

"No, look at me, Natalie! I don't care why you went. I don't give a goddamn about him. *Cara mia*, all I care about is you. About you and nothing else in the world." He tilted her chin up to look at him and the pain there skewered him. "*Cristo*, you're the most wonderful thing that has ever come into my life. The most joyful thing. The thing that Mama hoped I would find and nurture."

He kissed her soft cheek slowly, softly, breathing in

the scent of her. Looking for courage in the tension that swept through her body. "Forgive me for all the dirty accusations." A kiss at her temple. "Forgive me for not listening." A kiss on the tip of her nose. "Forgive me for putting the bloody contract before you." A kiss on her forehead. "Forgive me for not trusting you."

He dropped to his knees, anchoring his hands around her hips, burying his face in her belly. Pressed countless kisses to every inch of her he could touch and feel. He was shaking and he couldn't stop himself because he was still afraid he would never hold her like this.

He let the fear and the joy and the warmth gush through him, let himself breathe it in. Because this was what loving Natalie meant.

Embracing this…emotional storm. Embracing the fear. Embracing the fact that she'd make him weak and strong but better for it. And he let her see all the things he couldn't put into words in his eyes. "Forgive me, the most, for not trusting myself. Forgive me for not listening to the part of me that is worthy of you.

"Forgive me, *cara mia*, for not saying that I love you. Forgive me for being an arrogant bastard who couldn't see love when it kissed him on the mouth and held him in the night and told him there was a hero inside waiting to get out. *Ti amo*, Natalie. You make me a better man, *cara mia*. If you were with me I'd be the best of them all. The best Brunetti of all. And I'd maybe start a new trend of what it means to be a Brunetti, *sì*?"

Natalie fell into Massimo's waiting arms, the sob she'd been trying to bury bursting out of her chest. "I love you, too, Massimo, so much that it terrifies me. I… I've never loved anyone like that. I…want to trust this but—"

"Shh…*cara mia*. No, there's no place for fear or doubts between us. There's no place for anything but love." And then he was kissing her mouth, so softly, so tenderly, and Natalie fell into the kiss. His desperation, his relief, his warmth, his love—his kiss spoke of a thousand things and she took it all in. "Say you'll believe me, Natalie."

He had believed her when he had no reason to. Given her a chance to prove herself. She would give him a million chances, she realized, shaking with alarm, but whatever fear and doubts came at them, Natalie wanted to face it with him. Together. "I do believe you. I'm all in, Massimo."

"We'll bring Frankie here immediately. We'll build a home for ourselves. We'll start fresh, *cara mia*, with no shadows. And when you marry me—"

And just like that, Natalie fell in love a little more. "What?" Her heart thudded in her chest.

His eyes shining, Massimo slid his lips over hers in a silky caress. "When you marry me, we'll start our own brood of Brunettis and the first thing and the only thing we will teach them is—"

"How to be courageous in love," she finished, her eyes full of tears.

His teeth dug into his lower lip and he nodded. "So you will, *sì*?"

"*Sì*. You're my hero." He was so solid and warm and hard around her. "And you're all mine," she said, and he nodded, and when he pulled her into his lap and buried his hands under her shirt, looking for warm skin, she gave herself over to it.

He was her hero. Her man. Her entire life.

EPILOGUE

IF SOMEONE HAD told Natalie a few months ago, or even a few weeks ago, that she'd be walking down a beautifully manicured path with elegant trees and boxwood and wisteria on either side, while her little brother walked in front of her, toward a stunning vista of lakefronts and mountains in an ivory designer gown that supermodel Alessandra Giovanni had requested personally of a designer friend who never did private commissions, toward the tech billionaire Massimo Brunetti to make her wedding vows, she'd have laughed hysterically.

She'd have rolled on the floor, laughing her ass off.

No woman was so lucky to have a wedding at such a stunning location with the elements behaving perfectly as if they'd conspired to give her their best on her most important day.

No woman could be so selfish as to demand a designer gown that was yards and yards of lace and tulle that made even skinny little hackers look like a princess.

No woman would hope to have a kind, sexy, absolutely wonderful man waiting for her at the end, his heart in his eyes, looking knee-meltingly gorgeous in a black tuxedo.

No one in their right mind would at least guess that all of the above could happen to an orphan who'd never thought she was worthy of anything so wonderful.

But it was happening. Alessandra and Greta looked stunning on one side and Silvio and Leonardo on the other side, the latter with a warm smile for her that still stunned Natalie even after a month since she'd saved the Fiore project.

And then she was there, close to the man she adored with all her heart.

As she reached Massimo and he took his hands in hers and tugged her closer with a little too much enthusiasm that had the small, intimate crowd laughing, Natalie was trembling, sheer terror that it was all a dream that would disappear taking hold of her.

His fingers tight around hers, his breath whispering against her temple, Massimo said, "I have you, *cara mia*. You're the most beautiful woman I've ever seen and I love you so much, and whatever comes our way, we'll face it together, *si*?"

"I'm scared, Massimo. I love you so much and it robs the very breath from me when I think of our future and with—"

His finger covered her lips, the warmth of his body a comforting cocoon. "But I shall never, ever let you go. If you fall, I will always catch you. We will build our empire or take down someone else's if that's what you prefer, *si*?" he whispered, and Natalie laughed because this man knew her so well and each day he showed her what she meant to him.

She licked her lips, knowing that everyone was waiting. But God, she didn't want to start their life together with lies and shadows. "I wanted to tell you but I was afraid. Afraid that it would hurt you," she added quickly when she saw the light dim in his eyes. "This…this tiara—" she touched the exquisitely delicate diamond tiara wrought in the finest white gold that had been delivered three days ago sitting on top of the elaborate coif that her hair had been beaten into "—I… I didn't borrow it from Alessandra. I lied. Because I was worried you wouldn't understand.

"He…he sent it to me."

"I knew it, *bella*."

"What?"

"From the moment you opened the package and tried to hide the packing material and then burst into tears when you saw the card."

"Please don't be mad, Massimo. I've cut my association with him but he was still a big part of my life. He'll always be a big part of my past and I can't change it and I hate that I hid this from you—"

"I have long decided to forgive him, *cara mia*," he said, stealing the ground from under her. "I will help Leo find him, and stop him from causing further havoc in our lives, but how do I stay angry with a man who protected you when you were alone in the world? How long do I hate a man who gave me the most wondrous, beautiful gift of you? *Ti amo*, Natalie. Your past and your present, your stubborn but loyal heart, your fire and your flaws, I adore everything about you, *cara mia*."

Her tears plopped down her cheeks and Natalie didn't

give a damn if her makeup was ruined. "I love you, too, Massimo. Now, hurry up," she whispered against his mouth, "so that we can start building that empire and a brood of Brunettis."

His eyes glittered with wicked warmth and then the priest was admonishing them and Alessandra sighed and Frankie asked Leo in a loud whisper if they were going to kiss so frequently and then in the midst of the chaos and the love and the laughter, suddenly, she was now Natalie Brunetti.

And when Massimo took her mouth in a soft, tender kiss she lost her heart all over again.

* * * * *

If you enjoyed
An Innocent to Tame the Italian
by Tara Pammi,
you're sure to enjoy
Leonardo's and Vincenzo's stories
in The Scandalous Brunetti Brothers trilogy,
coming soon!

And why not explore these other
Tara Pammi stories?

Married for the Sheikh's Duty
Sheikh's Baby of Revenge
Sicilian's Bride for a Price

Available now!

Available July 16, 2019

#3737 THE ARGENTINIAN'S BABY OF SCANDAL
One Night With Consequences
by Sharon Kendrick

Housekeeper Tara is always professional. Until her billionaire boss, Lucas, looks at her with an intensity she just can't resist... Only now this innocent Cinderella has the task of flying to New York to tell him about the scandalous consequence!

#3738 THE MAID'S SPANISH SECRET
Secret Heirs of Billionaires
by Dani Collins

Sweet Poppy shouldn't have succumbed to aristocrat Rico's seduction, but his forbidden touch was all consuming... And it had a nine-month consequence! Now Rico's on her doorstep, demanding his hidden daughter and determined to make Poppy his wife!

#3739 AN HEIR FOR THE WORLD'S RICHEST MAN
by Maya Blake

To secure his latest deal, Joao needs his right-hand woman, Saffron. But a one-off, emotionally charged night together leads the tension between them to skyrocket...and then Joao discovers that Saffron is pregnant!

#3740 CONTRACTED AS HIS CINDERELLA BRIDE
Conveniently Wed!
by Heidi Rice

The perfect summer Ally spent with billionaire Dominic was unforgettable. But now Ally's a struggling courier, and she's stunned when her latest delivery brings her to Dominic's door. Yet what's even more shocking is his marriage proposal!

#3741 CLAIMING HIS ONE-NIGHT CHILD
Shocking Italian Heirs
by Jackie Ashenden

When Stella dramatically confronts playboy Dante over a family vendetta, he's intrigued...and enticed! Their attraction soon explodes into a sizzling encounter that leaves innocent Stella pregnant. Now, to claim his heir, Dante must marry this alluring woman...

#3742 PRINCE'S VIRGIN IN VENICE
Passion in Paradise
by Trish Morey

Prince Vittorio's invitation to hotel maid Rosa is supposed to end at Venice's Carnival ball. Yet their instant chemistry soon leads to a scorching encounter! But will one night with unexpected virgin Rosa be enough?

#3743 AWAKENED BY THE SCARRED ITALIAN
by Abby Green

Scarred and completely ruthless, Ciro is not the man Lara remembers. Yet their intense fire has never died, and his caress awakens untouched Lara to unimaginable pleasures. Could their convenient marriage be their redemption?

#3744 A PASSIONATE NIGHT WITH THE GREEK
by Kim Lawrence

Tycoon Zach has one mission: to track down the long-lost granddaughter of his mentor. But he quickly realizes that introducing feisty Katina to Greek society might be more trouble—and temptation—than he anticipated!

---

*Sweet Poppy shouldn't have succumbed to aristocrat
Rico's seduction, but his forbidden touch was all
consuming… And had a nine-month consequence!
Now Rico's on her doorstep demanding his hidden
daughter—and determined to make Poppy his wife!*

*Read on for a sneak preview of
Dani Collins's next story for Harlequin Presents,*
The Maid's Spanish Secret.

His arrival struck like a bus. Like a train that derailed her composure
and rattled on for miles, piling one broken thought onto another.

OhGodohGodohGod… Breathe. All the way in, all the way out,
she reminded herself. But she had always imagined that if this much
money showed up on her doorstep, it would be with an oversize
check and a television crew. Not him.

Rico pivoted from surveying her neighbor's fence and the
working grain elevator against the fading Saskatchewan sky. His
profile was knife sharp, carved of titanium and godlike. A hint of
shadow was coming in on his jaw, just enough to bend his angelic
looks into the fallen kind.

He knocked.

"Poppy…?" her grandmother prompted, tone perplexed by the
way she was acting. Or failing to.

How? How did he know? Poppy had no doubt that he did.
There was absolutely no other reason for this man to be this far off
the beaten track. He sure as hell wasn't here to see her.

Blood searing with fight or flight, heart pounding, she opened
the door.

The full force of his impact slammed through her. The hard angle
of his chin, the stern cast of his mouth, his wide shoulders and long
legs, and hands held in almost tense fists.

His jaw hardened as he took her in through mirrored aviators.
Their chrome finish was cold and steely. If he'd had a fresh haircut,

it had been ruffled by the wind. His boots were alligator, his cologne nothing but crisp, snow-scented air and fuming suspicion.

Poppy lifted her chin and pretended her heart wasn't whirling like a prairie tornado in her chest.

"Can I help you?" she asked, exactly as she would if he had been a complete stranger.

His hand went to the door frame. His nostrils twitched as he leaned into the space. "Really?" he asked in a tone of lethal warning.

"Who is it, Poppy?" her grandmother asked.

He stiffened slightly, as though surprised she wasn't alone. Then his mouth curled with disparagement, waiting to see if she would lie.

Poppy swallowed, her entire body buzzing, but she held his gaze through those inscrutable glasses while she said in a strong voice, "Rico, Gran. The man I told you about. From Spain."

There, she silently conveyed. *What do you think of that?*

It wasn't wise to defy him. She knew that by the roil of threat in the pit of her stomach, but she had had to grow up damned fast in the last two years. She was not some naive traveler succumbing to a charmer who turned out to be a thief, or even the starry-eyed maid who had encouraged a philandering playboy to seduce her.

She was a grown woman who had learned how to face her problems head-on.

"Oh?" Gran's tone gave the whole game away in one murmur. There was concern beneath her curiosity. Knowledge. It was less a blithe "Isn't that nice that your friend turned up?" More an alarmed "Why is he here?"

There was no hiding. None. Poppy might not be able to read this man's eyes, but she read his body language. He wasn't here to ask questions. He was here to confront.

Because he knew she'd had his baby.

Don't miss
The Maid's Spanish Secret,
available August 2019 wherever
Harlequin® Presents books and ebooks are sold.

www.Harlequin.com

HPEXP0719